The Silver Horse, Braised

A New Sherlock Holmes Mystery

Note to Readers:

Your enjoyment of this new Sherlock Holmes mystery will be enhanced by re-reading the original story that inspired this one –

The Adventure of Silver Blaze.

It has been appended and may be found in the back portion of this book.

THE SILVER HORSE, BRAISED

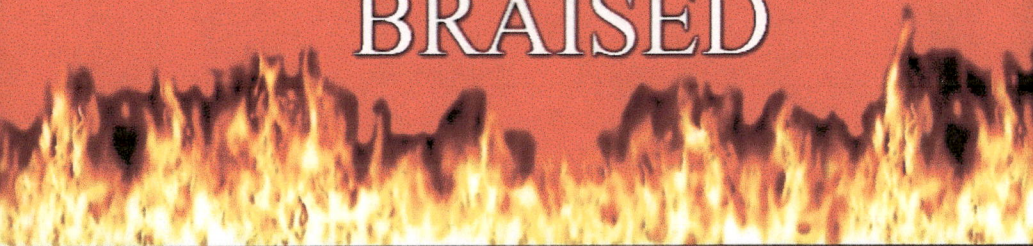

The Silver Horse, Braised

Braised

A New Sherlock Holmes
Mystery #15

Craig Stephen Copland

Published by:

Conservative Growth Inc.
3104 30th Avenue, Suite 427
Vernon, British Columbia, Canada
V1T 9M9

Cover design by Rita Toews.

ISBN 13: 978-1519269270

ISBN: 1519269277

Dedication

To the Toronto Bootmakers, the Sherlock Holmes Society of Canada. My attendance at their annual Silver Blaze Event at the Woodbine Racetrack in Toronto some years ago was my first participation in that wonderful worldwide network of splendid folks known as Sherlockians.

Welcome to New Sherlock Holmes Mysteries -

"The best-selling series of new Sherlock Holmes stories. All faithful to The Canon."

Each story is a tribute to one of the sixty original stories about the world's most famous detective. If you are encountering these new stories for the first time, start with *Studying Scarlet,* and keep going. (https://www.amazon.com/dp/B07CW3C9YZ)

If you subscribe to Kindle Unlimited, then you can 'borrow for free' every one of the books.

They are all available as ebooks, paperbacks, hardcovers, and in large print.

Check them out at www.SherlockHolmesMysteries.com.

Contents

Acknowledgments

All writers of pastiche stories of Sherlock Holmes must acknowledge their debt to Sir Arthur Conan Doyle and to the Sacred Canon of the original stories. Or, if you are a hopeless Sherlockian, then to Dr. John H. Watson, who wrote almost all of the stories, and that Doyle chap who was his literary agent and got *The Strand* to publish them.

This particular story, however, inspired as it is by *Silver Blaze,* concerns a race horse, and the finest writers of stories connected to the race track are Dick Francis and, before him and too far removed in time from the days of Sherlock Holmes, Damon Runyon. I have, therefore, borrowed Runyon's characters, made famous in the musical of *Guys and Dolls,* and integrated them into this mystery. I trust that Sherlockians will enjoy them and not be overly offended.

I first discovered *The Adventures of Sherlock Holmes* while a student at Scarlett Heights Collegiate Institute in Toronto. My English teachers – Bill Stratton, Norm Oliver, and Margaret Tough – inspired me to read and write. I shall be forever grateful to them.

My dearest and best friend, Mary Engelking, read all drafts, helped with whatever historical and geographical accuracy was required, and offered insightful recommendations for changes to the narrative structure, characters, and dialogue. Thank you.

Many words and whole phrases and sentences have been lifted and copied shamelessly and joyfully from the sacred canon of Sherlockian literature.

For the very idea of writing a new Sherlock Holmes mystery, I thank the Toronto Bootmakers, the Sherlock Holmes Society of Canada.

Chapter One

The Race is On

"**I** am afraid, Watson, that I shall have to go," said Holmes, as we sat down together to our breakfast one morning.

"Go? Where to?"

"Not far. Just over to Surrey; Epsom to be precise."

"Ah, I am not surprised. You have been called regarding the death of that poor jockey, have you? Or has some other crime been committed already, even before the Century Race has been run?"

Three days ago, the press had reported on the tragic death of one of England's greatest jockeys, Nester Leggatt. He had been on an early morning ride on top of Lord Commodore, one of the favorites to win the Century Race. While at full gallop, the horse had suddenly lurched, sending the jockey crashing into a furlong pole. He was dead by the time the other trainers and jockeys got to him. The horse's owner, Lord Biggleswade's oldest son, Baron Julian, had immediately called for an inquiry and set up a fund for the chap's family. He was duly admired for his prompt and compassionate action.

"No on both counts, my good doctor," replied Holmes." The death of Nester Leggatt is still ruled accidental, although Lestrade is, quite rightly, somewhat suspicious. But that event, combined with the silly disappearance of another favored jockey, has given rise to the imagining of every conceivable crime that could possibly take place before such an enormous event. Inspector Gregory is in Epsom and has requested my assistance, with the hope that we may be able to prevent such crimes before they happen. I do not object to assisting him. He is quite a bright police office even if lacking in imagination."

Officially the race was called the Wheatcroft Cup, but everyone was simply calling it *The Race of the Century*. It was scheduled three weeks after the Derby, was to be a one-time final event of the racing season in the last year of the glorious Nineteenth Century and was acclaimed as the final judgment on which country, England or America, bred the finest racehorses. A wealthy nobleman, Lord Wheatcroft of Cork, had offered an exceptional prize of twenty thousand pounds to the winner, with additional record-breaking prizes for place and show. Seven of the best five-year-olds from America had been brought across the Atlantic to compete with the seven top-ranked five-year-olds in England. It would be a once-in-a-lifetime opportunity to watch fourteen of the finest thoroughbreds in the world run against each other in what promised to be a breath-taking spectacle. The annual Derby at Epsom Downs was normally the climax event of the racing season, but this extraordinary one would surpass all that had come before.

Even the dear old girl herself, Our Gracious Queen Victoria, now in the sixty-second year of her reign, was invited. Some members of the press had promised that she would be there, Union Jack in hand, cheering on the Empire. The betting, Queen and Union Jack or not, had been terrific. The registered bookmakers had already taken in over one million pounds, and it was guessed that several times that amount had been wagered in the pubs and backrooms across all of Great Britain. In addition to that, we could not, in our wildest dreams, imagine how much had been laid down in America.

The combination of the spectacle, the amount wagered, the tragic death of the jockey, and the fact that Americans were involved had given rise to all sorts of rumors and speculation in the press about crimes that were in the works. Murders, abductions, threats, bribes, the administering of opiates to horse or rider, immoral seductions, and the circulation of false statistics had all been mentioned. Odd-looking characters had been spotted throughout London and Sussex, dressed in loud, gaudy short suit jackets, and speaking in a dialect of the Queen's English that was incomprehensible to an English gentleman.

For several days a story circulated through the populace, aided by it's being repeated in the press, that one of the nation's most successful jockeys, Bob Sockmaker, who had been assigned to ride an English favorite, Vindication of Yarmouth, owned by Lord Atherstone, had vanished. He had last been seen on the Saturday afternoon of a week ago while throwing back pints of ale at *Ye Olde King's Head* in the village of Epsom. Immediately it was suggested that he had been abducted by some American syndicate so that he would not be able to participate in the Century Race. Sherlock Holmes dutifully applied himself to the situation for a mere ten minutes before throwing down the newspaper and muttering, "Imbecilic nonsense. Anyone can see that he was three sheets of the wind. He will reappear when he is sober."

That was indeed what happened.

"How could you tell?" I asked, incredulously, as is often the case in my questions to Holmes.

"Elementary, Watson. The accounts in the various papers quote five different witnesses who say that they watched him down three or four pints of ale. All five claim to have been in the pub at different times on Saturday afternoon and evening, which means that at a minimum, Mr. Sockmaker drank fifteen to twenty pints. He is next thing to a midget in size and cannot weigh more than nine stone. By nine o'clock in the evening, he must have been blind drunk when he failed to return from yet another trip to the loo. I will guarantee that he passed out within a block or two of the pub and will return once he regains consciousness and finds himself a clean pair of knickers. My knowing this is nothing more than the application of the art of the reasoner."

He was right. But by the time the jockey reappeared the press, having had enough of dead and drunk jockeys, moved on to other rumors.

Our friends at Scotland Yard were normally immune to nonsensical reports, having heard every one imaginable over the past century. This time, however, they were erring on the side of caution since, after all, if Americans were involved, there was always a possibility of nefarious criminal activity. The inspectors' burning desire was to spot the most likely culprits and stuff them on a boat back across The Pond before their evil intents could be brought to fruition.

The fact that the Yard had requested the help of Sherlock Holmes was a strong indication that they had concluded that at least a few of the rumors might have substance to them.

"I should be most happy to go with you if I should not be in the way," said I.

"As my knowledge of horse racing is limited to knowing which end of the horse moves forward," said Holmes, in his habit of feigned modesty, "and since you are an avid sportsman, I should be most grateful for your invaluable help. And, by the way, I would you oblige me by bringing your very excellent field glasses."

And so it happened that an hour or so later I found myself in the corner of a first-class carriage flying along on route for Epsom, while Sherlock Holmes, with his sharp, eager face framed in his ear-flapped traveling-cap, dipped rapidly into the bundle of fresh papers which he had procured at the Victoria Station. He made his way through the *Chronicle,* the *Telegraph,* and *The Times.*

I concentrated my reading on *The Sporting News,* the tabloid followed religiously by all true sportsmen, those who were prepared to demonstrate their passionate commitment to sport by putting down a quid or two on the results. The histories of all fourteen racehorses were provided in detail, along with the odds offered on each. It was not surprising that the odds differed little from one horse to another, given that every one of them had a record of winning many races over the past three years. Every writer had made a case for his particular favorite, and they all disagreed with each other. I had given some consideration to placing a wager or two on the race, but given the shortening of the odds, I was inclined to refrain.

Although I was quite sure of the response I would receive, I could not resist engaging Holmes in the topic.

"What say, Holmes? Are you going to add to the excitement of our excursion by putting down a few quid on your favorite nag?"

He gave me a look that was not the dismissive glance I had expected but was rather on the thoughtful side. He said nothing for several minutes while he stuffed some strong black tobacco into his beloved pipe, lit it, breathed in, and gave a long and slow exhale.

"Men," he finally said quietly, "gamble to lose."

"Oh come, Holmes," I protested. "All of us, myself included, place our bets with the hope of winning."

"And you are fools in doing so. The fundamental arithmetic accuses you. The total winnings distributed to the lucky few must, of necessity, be less than the total amount bet. Otherwise, the gambling house, the bookmakers, the jockey club, the publican, and all others who make their income from the practice of gambling could not exist. The inevitable conclusion from such an observation is that any man with even a modest intellect knows that over time he must become poorer by gambling. Yet it is not the absurd stupidity of the institution that intrigues me, as an even more puzzling matter."

Here he stopped and gave a few more puffs on his pipe. I posed the obvious question.

"And what might that be?"

"That wherever gambling is taking place, crime invariably follows."

Epsom, in Sussex, is a pleasant little town in the North Downs, about fifteen miles south of London. It was famous first for its Epsom Salts and now, of course, for the Derby.

Holmes and I had both visited it several times over the past two decades, and I expected that we would take a cab immediately to our preferred hotel, The Chalk Lane, just north of the racecourse. Holmes had other plans. He directed the cabbie to take us straightaway to the scene of the crime, the racecourse. Once there, he made inquiries as to who it was who had witnessed the accident that led to the tragic death of Nester Leggatt. No one, it turned out, had actually seen what had happened, but we were sent to find a fellow named Robert Blinden, a stable boy who was first on the scene and found the body.

Blinden was said to be working in the large stable barn in which the horses that were to run in the Century Race were being kept. Armed guards and dogs were stationed outside the doors of the barn, and we were not permitted to enter. A message was sent in, and shortly afterward, a man appeared and walked toward us. I was immediately struck by his appearance. He was of average height and weight, but his head was overly large for his body. His face was excessively round and had I not known that he was gainfully employed, I would have taken him for a mongoloid, and mentally deficient.

He walked with his head down and, on meeting us, kept looking at his shoes while speaking. He confirmed that he had been the first witness to the tragedy. He had been working outside the barn when he looked over to the far side of the track and saw that one of the horses was riderless, and walking back and forth on the turf. He said he knew that something might be amiss and ran over to the horse, and it was then that he discovered the body of Nester Leggatt lying beside the track and already dead.

He imparted these few things as we walked across the fairgrounds that occupied the inner section of the racecourse. At the top of the hill, kitty-corner from the stands, he stopped and said, "Sir, this is where I found him. He was lying right here, Mr. Holmes."

"Now, my good man," said Holmes. "Might I ask you to think very hard and try to remember exactly what you saw when you arrived here? Could you do that for me?"

Holmes's tone of voice was of the sort that one might use when speaking to a child. The fellow responded, continuing to look at the ground in painful shyness.

"Yes sir, I can do that. And please, Mr. Holmes, I am not a child, and I am not stupid. Everybody thinks I am because of my big stupid face, but I know that there is nothing wrong with my brain. And sir, I have read every one of the stories that Dr. Watson has written about you. I've read them many times, sir. So I knew right off when I got here that something did not seem right, sir, and that I should try to look closely at as many little things as possible before a whole crowd of people got here and trampled all the evidence. I did try to do that, sir, just as I thought you would, had you been here, sir."

Holmes positively lit up with a smile. "Did you now, Robert? That is splendid. You fill me with interest, and you must tell me all that you observed. Should we be successful in solving this mystery, I am certain that Dr. Watson will give you all the credit you deserve. Is that not correct, Watson?"

I nodded vigorously. "Entirely correct, entirely."

Robert Blinden appeared for a moment or two to be nodding his head and moving his lips, perhaps rehearsing his unprecedented opportunity to be of assistance to his hero.

"The first thing I could see, sir, was the terrible mark on his neck. The constable who came later said that the half-furlong pole must of struck him in his neck and broken it, and that was why he was dead."

"Yes," said Holmes. "That does seem a reasonable conclusion, is it not?"

"Well, no sir, it was daft," said Blinden, now looking directly at Holmes. "The mark was straight across his neck, like this." He brought his hand straight across his neck in a gesture usually used for indicating the slicing of one's throat.

"Indeed," said Holmes. "Why do you say 'daft'?"

"Well, sir, I have worked at a racetrack now for over ten years, and I have seen a fair number of horses jolt, or fall, and their jockeys tumble. I have never seen a one where the jockey turned completely sideways in the air. They all tend to continue in the same position they were in, sir. They sort of jump off the horse and come forward with their head up and their feet down. Then they land, hitting the ground first with their feet, and they roll forward. That's how they come off their horses, sir. But poor Mr. Leggatt, sir, if the mark on his neck was from side to side, then he must have flipped sideways off the horse, and that just does not happen, sir."

Holmes nodded in appreciation. I scribbled notes diligently. I could see evidence of an accidental death diminishing.

"Continue, please, Mr. Blinden," said Holmes.

"Well, sir, when I was a schoolboy, I had to learn about Sir Isaac Newton and his laws. And I remembered that he said that if some object is moving in a certain way, then it keeps going in that same way. Isn't that right, sir?"

Holmes had only slightly more use for Newton than he did for Copernicus but nodded in the affirmative. Blinden continued.

"Well sir, I imagined that my left hand was Mr. Leggatt's head." He stretched out his left arm as he spoke and formed a fist with his hand. "And then my right hand would be his feet." He made a similar movement with his right arm and hand. "And if I were flying through the air sideways and my neck hits the pole, then my legs and feet would keep moving forward, would they not? Like this, sir."

He walked toward the pole so that his left wrist struck it, and then he pivoted around the pole, tracing an arc through the air, horizontal to the ground, with his right hand.

"Sir, that is how the body must of moved if he struck the pole with his neck. The body should have landed on the far side of the pole, with his feet the farthest away. Does that not seem right, sir?"

I spoke up. "It does indeed. But that is not where you found the body."

"No. It were on the near side, with his head up close to the pole and his feet pointing back to the start line. That made no sense, or at least, that is what I thought, sir."

"An excellent observation, my good man," said Holmes. "And was there anything else?"

"Well sir, as soon as I seen the poor fellow, I shouted and screamed back across the fairground, and quite a few other chaps were now running toward me. So, I did not have a chance to look at much more before they pushed me aside. But there was one other thing that I did notice."

"Yes, and what was that?" asked Holmes.

"Well sir, it was the first practice run of the morning, and the turf was a bit soft from the rain during the night. It was right easy to see the hoof prints of Lord Commodore. A big galloping racehorse leaves his mark on soft turf. So, I did a quick look just before all the rest of the fellows got here, and I could see the proofs in the turf. The horse was galloping full speed right up to the place where the jockey had come off. But then I looked, and there was no sign of the horse jolting; he just kept on galloping another thirty yards, and then he slowed and stopped. That made me wonder some more, sir. It all added up to be very suspicious. But by then, another dozen chaps were bending over Mr. Leggatt and checking his pulse, and shouting instructions about how to save his life even though it was rather clear that his neck was broken and he was dead and gone. So that was all I could observe, sir."

"I could not have done a better job myself," said Holmes. He gave the fellow a friendly clap on his shoulder. Blinden raised his face and beamed a smile back at Holmes.

"Now then," said Holmes. "You will know if you have read Dr. Watson's stories about me, that after a detective has gathered data, he must avoid conjecture and surmise and deduce all possible theories, using his reason alone to explain the facts, and then diligently work to eliminate those that are impossible. I suspect that you have formed a theory or two, have you not? Ah ha, I see by your smile that you have. Pray tell, what have you deduced?"

"Well sir, really only one," replied Robert, now looking sheepish but with a smile spread across his wide face. "I think that Nester Leggatt ran into a clothesline, if you know what I mean, sir."

"I do know, and that would be my leading hypothesis as well. It would appear that someone stood here, beside this pole, had a rope or wire attached to it, and pulled it taut just as Lord Commodore approached in full gallop, catching Nester Leggatt by the neck. But he would have to have a way of anchoring the cord to the pole at the correct height."

Holmes was speaking mostly to himself at this point and was gazing up toward the top of the pole.

"How tall," he asked Blinden, "is Lord Commodore?"

"He's average for a thoroughbred. About seventeen hands."

Holmes looked at me, clearly needing a translation.

"Five feet eight inches from hoof to withers. The jockey stands in the stirrups and leans forward. His neck would have been another foot and a half above the withers."

"Thank you, my good doctor," said Holmes. He took his glass out of his coat pocket and began to examine the side of the pole closest to the starting gate.

"Watson," he said while staring up at the pole. "It is terribly inconsiderate of me to ask, but could you possibly drop to one knee and allow me to use your other leg as a step stool?"

I did as requested. Holmes, balancing himself with a hand on the pole, pulled off one of his boots, placed his stockinged foot on my upper leg, and hoisted himself up to where he could see the higher section of the pole. Bracing himself with one hand, he extracted his glass from his pocket and examined a portion of the pole that was directly in front of his face. Having done so, he lowered himself back to the ground and donned his boot.

"As I expected," he said. "There is a fresh hole with a diameter of a quarter of an inch. Just that right size to have been formed by a lag bolt or a thick threaded hook."

He now turned to Robert Blinden. "Sir, you have been exceptionally helpful. Now I must make yet another request of you."

"I am very pleased to help, Mr. Holmes."

"You must not say anything about what you have shown me. Not to anyone. It must remain a secret between us. Could I count on you to do that, sir?"

"Oh, of course, you can, Mr. Holmes. Helping Sherlock Holmes in solving a mystery is something I always dreamed of but never thought it might ever happen."

Again, he was smiling uncontrollably, but he then added, "It is very kind of you to ask me, sir, but in truth, no one would ever think I knew anything anyway. So keeping a secret is not a difficult thing to do when no one thinks you know anything."

We walked back toward the stable barns where we bade good-day to Robert Blinden. Having done so, Holmes turned to me.

"My good doctor, I must confess that I was as guilty as the next man in thinking that fellow was not particularly bright based only on the configuration of his face. If nothing else ever comes from this case, the lesson I have learned will be invaluable. Should you ever see me making such a foolish blunder again, you may whisper 'Epsom Downs' into my ear."

We then took ourselves to the inn. I had feared that it would be entirely occupied, given the excitement of the Century Race on the weekend, but the innkeeper, who immediately recognized Sherlock Holmes, was eager to provide us a suite. Once we had settled in, we proceeded to the dining room in search of some lunch.

As we entered, we were followed by three men who joined us at the same table. It was immediately obvious that they were Americans who had, I assumed, come to participate in the excitement that was abounding for the Century Race. By English standards, their appearance was outlandish. The tallest of them, towering more than a head above Holmes, was attired in a garish suit that bore wide colorful stripes, alternating among red, white, and blue. He did not so much as walk to the table as lope along with extended bobbing strides. The second fellow, somewhat on the portly side and with eyes that were distinctly puffy and melancholy, was wearing an elegant black suit with strong white pinstripes. Although somewhat loud by English taste, it might have been overlooked had it not been for the massive red and white polka-dotted bowtie that graced the top of a starched white shirt. The third man, of average height and weight, similar in many respects to my own, was shamelessly wearing a bright yellow short suit jacket and matching trousers. His shirt was black, and his long necktie a somewhat lighter shade of yellow. My immediate thought on looking at this strange set of visitors was that that they must, at all costs, be kept away from the racecourse for fear of terrifying the horses.

"Gentlemen," said the chap in the yellow suit, as he reached across the table to shake first my hand and then Holmes's. "You seem to me to be more than somewhat interested in the sport of kings, else why would you be in this two-bit burg on a pleasant autumn morning? As my esteemed colleagues and I have similar preoccupations allow me to introduce Mr. Harold Stanley Vincent Corrigiano Jr., but as that moniker is more than somewhat of a mouthful, he is known by all and sundry as Harry-the-Horse. Beside him, on your left, which is his right is Mr. Archibald Jones, better known, because of his disposition, as Sorrowful. And who, may I be so bold as to inquire, am I addressing in the persons of you two fine gentlemen?"

Without thinking, I responded. "My colleague is Mr. Sherlock Holmes, and I am Dr. John Watson."

The loquacious chap's face took on a rather surprised look, and for a second, he seemed nonplused, but he recovered quickly and responded. "Ordinarily, I do not care to doubt the word of a gentleman, but do you really mean to tell me that you are the one and only Mr. Sherlock Holmes, the world's most famous detective?"

"Huh?" interjected the tall chap who had been introduced as Harry-the-Horse. "Are you thinking that there are maybe two of them?"

"There is only one of them," muttered the Sorrowful fellow quietly. "That's him, alright. He is looking just like the guy in the pictures of the stories I read at bedtime to the kid. Yeah, that's him."

Holmes, who did not seem to be interested in a conversation with these fellows, nodded as he poured himself a cup of coffee. "I am he."

"I must say," returned the man who I was now sure was not only an American but most likely from New York City. "It is not my practice normally to have any truck in any manner, shape, or form with a detective, as all of those I have known who belong to that profession are much too closely aligned with the local constabulary. But it is a privilege and a pleasure to make the acquaintance of so famous a citizen of England, about whom I would no doubt have read had I been in the habit of reading books."

Harry turned and, in a tone that was far from friendly, spoke to Holmes. "So Mr. Famous Detective, if a detective comes to a horserace, it means that the coppers or somebody thinks that the race is fixed. Since we have some serious duckets invested in this race, it would be a very good thing for your well-being if you were to tell me real fast if the fix is in for this big race. And I mean real fast 'cause I don't want my coffee to get cold."

I have known Sherlock Holmes now for many years. I knew that he did not take kindly to being threatened and could normally be counted on to give a sharp reply to anyone who so dared. I was quite sure that he was about to do so, and I had visions of having to depart the room before the food, which I was looking forward to, had arrived at our table. To my considerable surprise, however, Holmes smiled warmly in response.

"Ah, please sir, then let me warm up your cup of coffee and inform you that I am a private, consulting detective, representing the interests of a client who, as I am quite certain is the same for your clients, does not wish his identity to be known. He has a very strong interest in the race and only desires that any possible infractions of proper regulations be avoided."

Holmes reached for the pitcher of coffee and topped up the tall fellow's cup.

"I get it," Harry continued. "Your client is worried that someone might put the fix in, and you got to make sure it doesn't happen. Is that what you're telling me, Mr. Detective?"

"Precisely," replied Holmes, not bothering to add that his client was Scotland Yard. He then continued in a friendly and engaging manner. "I must, however, confess, gentlemen, that I fear my client has made a poor use of his funds by sending me here. My knowledge of horse races is exceptionally limited. My special province is the application of logical synthesis to complex and diabolical crimes. What possible connection could there be of a horse race to murders, assaults, kidnappings, and international intrigue? I doubt I will find any of that here and am most likely to be on the train back to London by this evening."

The three Americans looked at each other, briefly at me, and then back at Holmes. Harry spoke up. "So no offense, Mr. Detective, but in the neighborhood where I come from, I am supposing that you might be what we would call a chump. You know, one of those guys who do not know what time it is or even how to wind his watch. For a famous guy, you do not seem to be at all acquainted with horse racing."

"As I have never been in your neighborhood," replied Holmes, smiling, "It does not make any difference to me what I might be called. However, I can see nothing in horse racing other than lining up a group of large animals ridden by small men, racing them around a circle, and giving a bit of money to the winner. For the life of me, I cannot see why grown men would watch it eight times over in an afternoon and then return the next day to see it again. Why, it is no more than a childish way to waste time in the hope of winning a few shillings."

The look of offense combined with astonishment on the three faces was amusing, and it was all I could do to keep a straight face.

"Well now, Mr. Holmes," said the fellow in the yellow suit, "pardon me if I am by no means impressed with the state of your enlightenment. It so happens that this childish pastime has more than ten million bucks associated with it already, depending on the outcome of this big race alone, and the three men with whom you are sitting are in charge of over one million greenbacks, with which we are entrusted to invest on behalf of our clients in this running around a circle, as you call it."

Holmes, in well-practiced feigned surprise, gasped. "Good heavens. Why, that's enough money to start a war. All sorts of terrible crimes have been committed for much less than that. Please, gentlemen, please, allow me to provide you with a pleasant lunch and some excellent English ale if you will enlighten me concerning this enterprise of yours. How is it possible that it could attract a criminal conspiracy? Wherein could there ever be a crime?"

They seemed quite amenable to the prospect of a generous lunch and copious amounts of beer if Holmes was paying the bill, and they smiled back at him.

"I perceive, sir," said the man in the yellow suit, who appeared to be the ringleader of the trio, "that you are an excellent person who, most unfortunately, has not experienced the joy of a winning streak at a racetrack, which I will lay you six to five, is one of the finest experiences of high exhilaration available to all of mankind. It is all well and good that a horse should win a race and his owner and rider be rewarded, but it is the wagering of a C-note or two that elevates the experience to that which, in just over one minute, can render you either a comfortable man of means or one who is deeply financially embarrassed. Truly, sir, in the great and grand scheme of things, it matters not who won or lost, but on whom your bet was placed."

"Ah, yes. I see," said Holmes, all wide-eyed and innocent, "but how does a criminal become involved?"

"Allow me to enlighten you, sir," came the response. "Let us suppose that some guy is highly intent on impressing some gorgeous doll, and he deduces that he will need thirty G's with which to pay her rent on Park Avenue, and buy her a fur coat and a few diamonds if there is ever to be a chance that she will give him the time of day. But the most scratch he can come up with, after borrowing and leaving markers with all his friends and relatives, is ten G's. So he takes his ten G's to the track because he hears that a certain nag is a dark horse and truly very fast, and the odds being offered are five to one against that the nag will ever win the race. So, he lays his ten G's down on the nag to win. If it wins, then he collects fifty G's and he has enough to have the doll fall for him and still has his ten with which to pay back his friends, who are holding his markers, and the rest with which he can afford to eat at Delmonico's. He is now a happy man.

"I am most certain sir, that you will agree that this man is very motivated to do anything he can to make sure that his nag comes in a winner, as he cannot afford to lose both his borrowed scratch and the doll, which he will unless his horse wins. He now has a very strong incentive to take action. Such action might, from time to time, cross the line of what is considered to be strictly legal if you know what I mean."

"I am terribly sorry, my good man," returned Holmes, "but I fear I am all in the dark about what you mean. Kindly enlighten me."

"Well, it is like this. There are several courses of action, each with different odds available to him. The guy could offer a C-bill to each of the other jockeys to pull their mounts and slow down so his horse can win. Some elements of society would call such an action bribery, but the more progressive agree that it is simply another form of giving a decent working stiff a generous tip for a job well done. However, we do not consider it to be a wise tactic if there are more than a few horses in the race, as a guy will soon be out of C-Bills and have nothing left over to give to his bookie."

"Ah, yes," said Holmes. "That would present a somewhat prohibitive barrier unless one already had an abundance of money to start with."

"More than somewhat. If a guy already had enough scratch to tip every one of the jockeys, then he already has enough scratch for a doll and does not need any more anyway."

"I suppose," said Holmes, looking quite speculative, "that threats could be made to do violence to the other jockeys if they tried to win."

"Yeah," added Harry. "Or he could bump them off, which guarantees they cannot win, but he has to get rid of them all, and that does not usually work. The coppers get suspicious when a dozen jockeys all of a sudden up and die within three days before a big race. So we learn to avoid that tactic."

"Or," continued the first chap, "he could try to find another way to make all of the jockeys ride poorly, such as doping them before the race. But the practicalities of such an endeavor tend to be highly daunting."

"Indeed?" asked Holmes. "And why is that?"

"Unlike a horse, a jockey tends to express his displeasure if you stab him with a needle and administer a seven percent solution of cocaine, which will make him too stupid to win. If you feed him abundant quantities of powdered opium with his porridge and by chance give more than somewhat too much and he falls off the horse, then suspicions arise. So neither we nor any of our associates can be bothered to use that method."

"Quite so," said Holmes, taking this all in. "I presume that if you cannot affect the race by making arrangements of any type with the jockeys, then you have no choice but to make an arrangement with the horses."

"Now you are talking horse sense, Mr. Sherlock. If you are going to make an arrangement with the horses, you have one of three ways. The first two will slow a horse down, and the last will speed him up. Number one is done surgically by taking a small scalpel and giving the beast a nick in his Achilles tendon. This will work somewhat efficaciously as the horse will walk and canter normally, but when he comes to gallop, it begins to hurt, and he slows down. A week later, he is all better and back to normal. However, a spirited racehorse is not fond of having someone stick a knife in his fetlock. It is not long ago that we hear of some guy who tries to do this only to have his horse give him a very solid kick to his noggin and now he is looking at daisies from the bottom side up.

"The second means by which a fast horse can be made into a slower horse is by doping the animal. Just a bit of morphine given with a needle makes the beast happy for several hours, just like it does for a guy, and he does not feel like exerting himself, and so he does not.

"Of course, Mr. Sherlock, you are no doubt deducing the problem with trying to slow down a horse, on account of because in order to be sure that the horse on which you are betting places in the money, you have to make sure that almost every other horse is slower, which is a difficult thing to do in the few hours available to you before a race.

"So the method which we of the racing fraternity recommend is that if you are going to dope a horse, you first pick a more than somewhat fast horse and you dope him to win. You can make a horse run faster by giving him a small snort of opium, which makes the poor beast just a little bit stupid and not feeling any pain. So, he runs his heart out because he does not know that he is tired and should not keep going at full gallop over a long course. Now when you do this, sometimes the horse ups and dies after it crosses the finish line, and this is not looked upon happily by the officials or the owners, not to mention the horse. But once in a while, you can get away with it.

"Of course, an experienced man of the race track does not have to dope the animal himself on account of because all he needs is to know that a certain horse has been doped to win. This knowledge is what we, therefore, call the inside dope. If you have the inside dope on a good horse that is running at three to one or better, and that has been nicely doped, then you can place a bet with the expectation of making a good return on your investment.

"So that, and perhaps a bit more of this as well as that, Mr. Sherlock-the-Detective, is what a criminal can do with respect to a horse race. And if the criminal is smart, he can end up with a lot of potatoes in his pockets if you know what I mean."

"And may I assume," continued Holmes, "that you have made an extensive study of the situation here in Epsom and have determined whether or not any of the criminal actions you have described have taken place?"

"Yeah," said Harry. "We are looking it all over, and we ain't seeing nothing."

"We are informed," continued the first chap, "when we are in America that all the coppers over here in merry old England do not even arm themselves with anything more than a nightstick. Now we think this is not a very smart thing to do because if some guy is sticking up a jug and has a Roscoe in his hand and one in his pocket, a copper with a billy club is not much good, as the crook will not likely stand still and wait for the copper to knock him on the noggin. But when we are arrived in England, we find that we are badly misinformed, because all the stables at this here track in which the participating horses are kept are all guarded by coppers who have a Roscoe sticking out of both pockets, and a martini rifle slung across their backs, a twelve gauge in their arms, and a big nasty puppy at their feet. These are serious looking coppers who are not about to tolerate any tomfoolery, and the stables are locked up tighter than a nun's pajamas if you know what I mean. So the chances of getting inside and doping your favorite horse are somewhere between nil and squat. And we are surveying the stables for more than a week, and no one is getting inside them who does not belong."

"Well, that is good to hear," said Holmes. "but what about the jockeys? Have any of them been bribed?"

"Nope," said Harry. "We are looking at them real close, and we ain't seeing nothing."

"Those boys," said the first fellow, "are locked away like they just got off the boat at Ellis Island, and someone says they have the yellow fever. The one guy who gets loose is such a rube that he goes and gets drunk and would have been thrown out of the race had it not been that the magistrate is his pal and was drinking with him, but not as much. So, no sir, it does not look like anyone is getting to the jockeys. As a matter of fact, it would appear that this big race is going to be the cleanest of any big race we have ever had the pleasure of honoring with our presence."

Holmes nodded sagely and ordered another round of ale and meat pies, to be accompanied by mash, gravy, mushy peas, and a choice of either Stilton or Cheddar. Our American acquaintances, who were proving to be an excellent source of information for Holmes, tucked into the food and kept responding readily to Holmes's questions.

"Very well," continued Holmes, "if there is no inside dope, then would I be correct to presume that you will not be placing any bets on the race, and will simply enjoy the spectacle and return home?"

"That, Mr. Sherlock the Detective, is not an option that is open to us, for we have been entrusted with serious amounts of scratch from some guys in America who not only have a lot of potatoes but have friends with Roscoes who could make us very hard to find if we do not deliver on their requests. So even if the odds on the race cannot be assisted in being misleading, we face odds of three to one that our return to New York will be unpleasant if we do not bring back more than somewhat of the scratch with which we were entrusted."

"Might I prevail upon you," said Holmes, very earnestly, "to allow me to order some of our excellent deserts. I do believe that they serve a splendid trifle here, of the fortified variety. And while we are enjoying it, I would be most fascinated to hear the story of how it is that you have come to Epsom."

The three men looked at each other, obviously pondering Holmes's request. Mr. Sorrowful spoke up. "May as well. No offense Doc, or Sherlock, but you seem like far too cheap to be even thinking about placing a bet that would be big enough to shift the odds. And we suspect that you are too much of a rube to ever come to New York or even Philly and create consternation for us. So, sure, we can tell you our story." He directed his final comment to the chap in the yellow suit.

Chapter Two

The Parade Past

"It all begins," said the man in the yellow suit, "when I am sitting in Mindy's on Broadway minding my own business, reading the *Jockeys' Journal,* and eating an excellent beef stew. Mindy's, as you are not likely informed, has the best beef stew at a reasonable price in all of Midtown, which is not to say that the stew at Toots's is not also excellent, but the price is somewhat less than reasonable.

"As I am sitting there in walks a guy I know who we all know by the name of Fleagal Steigel. Perhaps his real name is something like Fred, but because he is a lawyer, he is known by all and sundry as Fleagal, on account of because of his occupation. Now he is not just any lawyer. He has a well-earned reputation for keeping his clients out of the sneezer, or if they do happen to find themselves such wise inconveniently detained, then getting them out of the sneezer. As a result, of which he has many close friends who are not to be messed with and best to be avoided.

"I immediately raise the *Journal* up in front of my face because I do not wish to have a conversation with Fleagal Steigel, for I have learned, as have my esteemed colleagues, that such a conversation most often does not end well for the guy who is on the recipient end of Mr. Steigel's communications. But I am not fast enough.

"'Ah ha, there you are,' says Fleagal Steigel, and he is walking in the direction of my table. Now the last words any guy wants to hear from a lawyer is 'Ah ha, there you are' unless, of course, he is your lawyer, but if he is your lawyer it is usually you who has to go looking for him and not vice-a versa if you know what I mean. 'I am happy to see you,' he says. I am thinking that I should say to him that that makes one of us who is happy, and it is not me, but I refrain since I do not wish him to become unhappy to see me.

"'Have you ever been to England?' he says to me. Now it is never good to look like you are too smart when talking to a lawyer, so I say 'Which England?' and try to keep looking not as smart as a lawyer. So he says, 'Are there two of them, and nobody has told me? The only England. The one on the other side of the ocean, next door to Europe.' I am tempted to ask, 'Which Europe?' but I refrain since it is already established that he is smarter than I am, and so I just say 'No.'

"Next, he wishes to determine that I am not currently overly encumbered by a situation of employment, which I assure him that I am not and have no immediate plans of becoming so encumbered. And then he asks if any of my esteemed colleagues are likewise unencumbered, and I say that maybe one or two of them also enjoy such liberty. And he says that is good news and would I mind terribly waiting in Mindy's because he has a client who would wish to speak to me and provide me and my colleagues with some temporary contractual obligations to which there will be a serious pecuniary reward attached. I say to him that I could perhaps spare a few minutes of my time before rushing off to my next engagement, which is not entirely true since there are no races on Sunday, and he says this is good and takes the wind and I have not seen him since that day.

"But about twenty minutes later, while I am still minding my own business and reading the *Journal,* but having finished my excellent beef stew and slowly enjoying my coffee, in walks a very odd-looking guy if I do say so, and he comes over to my table and sits down. And he likewise says that he is happy to meet me. He speaks excellent English except that it is distorted by an uppity English accent, and he is dressed unlike any man of business in New York and looks like a chump who wants to be a dandy, but he must have some serious potatoes because his suit, though odd, is not cheap or even close. In his one eye, he has a monocle, and he is squinting at me with his other. I refrain from any rejoinder about being or not being likewise happy, as now my interest is engaged, and I am thinking that Fleagal Steigel has acquired a client who might be able to pay me and my esteemed colleagues some scratch, which all of us are never too proud to turn down.

"He introduces himself and says that his name is Sir Clement Chenerton and he hails from London but has been living in America for the past ten years, mostly in Miami. And I should feel free to call him by his first name, which I take to be 'Sir.' He has a very exclusive business, he says, that involves moving funds back and forth, and most likely sideways I am thinking, between England and America. And he has a very special transfer of funds for which he needs personal service delivery, and I have been recommended for such an undertaking.

"Now I have learned not to look too eager when a guy, especially a foreigner who has been here for ten years but has not learned how to dress properly, asks you to do something special. And I say to him that there is an office of Western Union at the corner of West 51st and they are very good at sending funds to England or even to a god-forsaken place like Wisconsin, so why does he not make use of their services? He says that it is of utmost importance that all transactions remain confidential, which, although he does not exactly say so, I take to mean that it is important that it be kept confidential from the guys at the Infernal Revenue.

"And then he leaves me pretty well gobsmacked when he says that he needs to move over a million bucks across the ocean and back again, and he will pay me and my colleagues twenty G's for this service. I may perhaps have looked more than somewhat of an unbeliever, and so he pulls from his pocket a fat wad of G-notes and peels off twenty of them and slides them across the table and under my *Journal*, in which I now am no longer interested. I am wanting to play just a little hard to catch even if I am no longer so inclined, and I ask him how he knows that I will not just take his twenty G's and go to 'Frisco instead of London.

"He says that he is fully confident because I have excellent references, by which I take it to mean he is speaking of Fleagal Steigel and all those guys who are no longer in the sneezer. Therefore, I assure him that I am indeed such a man as he describes. And what, I ask, do we have to do with all the scratch he is entrusting to us? He says that there are many English guys, 'chaps' he keeps calling them, living in Florida because of the climate, which I understand to mean the climate of England not of Florida, but still have strong patriotic feeling towards old girl, Miss Vickie, the Queen, and out of loyalty are wanting to place very large wagers on this very big race that is coming up soon. He says that he sees an excellent opportunity and that, for a fee, he will look after placing their bets for them since he says he has a connection that will provide him with the inside dope, and so all of his chaps will receive *copias pecunias* in return. The chaps in Florida, who are tired of the small potatoes at Hialeah, are quite enthusiastic and before he knows it he has over one million smackers, but now he has to find a way to get the inside dope, which it seems he was more than somewhat short of having, and so he is referred to me by his friend, by which he means his lawyer, Mr. Fleagal Steigel, and he wishes to send me over to England first to find out the inside dope and then to place appropriate wagers accordingly. And furthermore, he expects that we will return with an additional one million dollars at least and that ten percent of whatever is honestly earned shall be ours to keep. Now ten percent is a significant cut of the proceeds and would amount to a hundred G's just for spending a couple of weeks of having to drink warm beer and getting seasick. So I agree, and I go and recruit my esteemed colleagues, who are sitting here with you. We three have acquired a reputation for expertise in discerning the inside dope at all of the better race tracks in New York, Philly, Chicago, and Miami, and so we are quite confident that we can do the same in England, since, after all, they do speak some version of the English language, and are said to raise excellent horses. We board a ship, and now we are here."

"Yeah," said Harry. "But it has been a bust. A total bust."

"Oh my," said Holmes. "That must be terribly disappointing. I am so sorry to hear that. But if you cannot return empty-handed, what are you going to do?"

"I would not wish to appear to be pompous, pretentious, or otherwise putting on airs as if I were a Yaley," said the man in the yellow suit, "but when there is no inside dope to be had then those of us who apply ourselves diligently as handicappers in the sport of kings have no alternative but to make use of what I call the science of deduction."

I felt a smirk coming on, but kept a straight face and concentrated on continuing to take notes.

"I am familiar with that term," said Holmes, "although not in the context in which you appear to be using it. Kindly explain, sir."

By this time, Holmes and I had moved on to brandies. Our American visitors demanded that the barkeep bring them "Jack and water" and, fortunately, the inn, having been warned of an influx of punters from across The Pond, was well supplied with their beverage of choice. Holmes lit up his pipe and sat back. The three across the table lit cigarettes and drank their whiskeys rather more quickly than I thought good for their internal constitutions, and then ordered another round.

Sorrowful and Harry continued to say very little, leaving it up to their verbose ringleader.

"I agree," confirmed Holmes. "Pray continue. I am all attention."

"Well sir, when it comes to applying the science of deduction to handicapping horse races, the first not so little a thing is to know the age of the horses, there being a great difference between a race for three-year-olds at the start of the season and a race for five-year-olds at the end of the season. We, my esteemed colleagues and I, do not stoop to the unseemly, inhumane, and highly unethical practice of supporting races of two-year-olds, as such races are a distaste to all devotees of true horse racing since they are not good for the young animals, and so we have nothing to do with them unless we have a contractual obligation to one of our clients to place his bets, and then we make an exception. However, when a maiden racehorse appears at the track for his first race, there is one little thing that is of great importance, and it is his bloodline, his pedigree. Who sires him? Who is his daddy, so to speak? And to a lesser extent, his dam. If there is no record of any previous races, then it is of great importance that you know if his sire is a winner or a loser. If he comes from a strong bloodline, then you can count on his being a good horse, and you can usually agree to six to five in his favor. If his sire is a dud, then it is more than somewhat likely that he will be as well.

"In addition to the bloodline, you now have to look at where your horse placed in all the races in which he runs. Does he win through his conditions and move up to higher races? And then you look at which racetrack those races took place. And who is the jockey? And who are the other horses? And does he run on a cold day or a hot day? Does he run best on turf or dirt? And is it raining buckets in the days preceding the race making the turf like mud, or is it dry for two weeks so that the grass is as hard as cement? And then you have to respect the opinions of the handicappers and the bookmakers and pay attention to their morning line because they make their living on getting a lot of data and setting the odds accordingly. Now, of course, they will not all agree with each other. But it is a difference of opinion that makes horse races, so you have to make your judgment and place your bets according to all the data and the opinions of others who are likewise placing bets.

"Now then, in a race where there is a favorite, and you are in agreement that this horse is sure to win then, you may go ahead and bet on him to win. But if you are not certain, then it is better to bet on him to place or show since by doing so, you increase the odds of getting something even if you decrease the odds of winning more than just something. If you are a skilled and scientific handicapper, you will govern your feelings and not place wild bets on long odds. You will instead place bets to place or show on horses for which the odds are not as exciting because that is the way you win more often than you lose."

"Oh," said Holmes. "I am always reading news of dark horses that surprised everyone by winning at twenty to one. Why not bet on those?"

"It is true, as the good book says, that the battle is not always to the strong nor the race to the swift. But that's the way you bet. Allow me, sir, to tax you with some scientific arithmetic. If you bets are all at twenty to one and if in one race out of a hundred a horse wins at twenty to one, then it is a truly certain thing that for every dollar you win, you will lose four. If you keep doing that, you are either a rich young guy who is doing this to impress some doll, or you are a dumb chump on your way to the poorhouse."

"A point well taken," said Holmes, nodding his now enlightened approval. "Now, please permit me to beg your indulgence, and may I ask if you might be willing to advise me on how to lay my bets for the Century Race? I fear I am blind as a mole on my own."

The three Americans again looked at each other and then the chap in the yellow suit shrugged his shoulders. "As you have been to us a gracious and generous host, it is appropriate that we return the favor. May I suggest that you, Doc, take notes while we share with you our enlightened insights.

"I must, however," he continued, "preface my remarks but affirming that each one of us are not only loyal flag-waving Americans, true to the Red, White, and Blue, we are also indeed Republicans, and so it grieves us to admit to you our inevitable conclusions. Allow me first to impart our insights on our fine American horses.

"Each of us," he said, "has a strong emotional attachment to one or more of the American horses. Harry would love to bet all his ducats on the horse named Paul Revere, since he knows that when the weather's clear, and the track wet that this horse cannot lose since he likes mud. Sorrowful, on the other hand, has had many very joyful days at Aqueduct by placing his bets on Valentine, for whom the morning line is almost always giving odds of five to nine. The horse has a chance at the big race, according to the jockey's second cousin, who is a friend of mine. My bets would have been placed on Epitaph, who according to the *Telegraph,* is the great-grandson of Equipoise, and the class of his pedigree is nothing at which to be sneezed. So, if we were placing our bets on American horses and betting with our hearts, it would be on those. However, a man who bets with his heart instead of his head is a man who is soon out of ducats and back living with his mother. Therefore, we are doing some scientifically serious handicapping and deducing, and we are of the conclusion that if you are going to bet on an American horse, then your bets should be on Clam, who two years ago wins the Preakness and wins a dozen or more stakes races since that time. He is the best of the lot, although we are not fond of him personally on account of because his owner, Mr. Montague Quimson-Filmore, says many unkind things about the proud fraternity of handicappers."

"Ah," said Holmes, "looking very much enlightened, "so the smart money is on Clam."

"Nah," said Sorrowful. "It would be, but this big race is not exactly fair. The odds are stacked in favor of the limeys."

"I beg your pardon," said Holmes, looking quite indignant. "You have already said that you found no possible criminal fix. How can you say the race is not fair?"

"We are led to believe," continued the chap in the yellow suit, "that a racecourse is a racecourse is a racecourse. Some are sprint courses and less than a mile. Others, by which I mean almost all the rest of them, are one mile long, made out of an oval, and flat. The longest race our horses run is the Belmont, which is a mile and four furlongs."

"Ah yes," I piped up. "This race is a Cup course and is to be run on the long track; over two miles, and it has the long hill up and then down."

"That, Doc, is what we are now knowing. It is bad enough that our dearly beloved favorites are spending a week on a boat without proper exercise, without which a horse forgets how to run, but our colts do not run truly long courses. Your English horses, on the other hand, are highly experienced in running for a long time on turf. It is like they are playing ball in their home field. They have a distinct advantage of a more than somewhat amount, meaning that no matter how much we wave the flag for our all-American champions, your English horses are going to show their heels to our American steeds, even to our best of the best, the horse that goes by the name of Clam."

"All very useful to know," said Holmes. "You have instructed me as to which horse I should not bet on, but you have given me no enlightenment as to which you have deduced most likely to win."

"Well now, sir, it goes like this. Before getting on the boat to come over here, I visit my old pals, Patience and Fortitude at their pad looking out over Fifth Avenue, and make my way up to Rosie's Room and ask for all the back copies of your *Sporting News,* so that I am able to do my due diligence and a serious handicapping on all your English horses. The lady librarian, who is of a certain age but still a doll, if you like your dolls that age, and at our age, we have no choice but to do so; she finagles out of me what I am looking for, and to my considerable surprise she not only fetches me the back copies of your newspapers but she tells me that the safe money is being bet on Lord Commodore and Vindication of Yarmouth. I do not know how she knows this, but it seems her dear departed uncle is a successful handicapper, originally from Dublin. But then she says to me, real on the quiet, that I should look at this horse who goes by the name of Mr. Silver and ridden by none other than Donny Cotter."

"The ghost horse of Westbury," I exclaimed. "He is quite the mystery, I must say."

"So, Doc, it would appear that you are familiar with this horse and that he is quite the enigma to a handicapper."

"Good heavens, Watson," interrupted Holmes. "What do you mean, a *ghost* horse?"

The chap in the yellow suit gestured to me to pick up the story. "There is some confusion about his pedigree," I said, not entirely sure of myself. "He was brought four years ago to Colonel Ross by a group of Gypsies. They said that they had found a young colt wandering all by himself in the wooded hills between Westbury and Bratten. He was completely white in color. Not a spot of any other markings anywhere. The Gypsies were quite convinced that he was the supernatural offspring of the Great White Horse of Westbury and the long-necked White Horse in Cherhill."

"The Roma people," Holmes observed, "are to be complimented on their skill in sales, especially when dealing with gullible gentry. Pray, continue."

"Colonel Ross made inquiries all over Salisbury and Wiltshire, but no stable reported losing a pure white colt. He purchased it from the Gypsies and gave it to his trainers to see if it had any potential as a racehorse. I do not know much more about it as it has not been run in very many races, and those it has run in are mostly long cup races, and its bloodline is completely unknown."

"This is what we learned as well," said the chap in the yellow suit. "We read all the old copies of your *Sporting News* as well as the *Daily Racing Form* for every day and at every course in which he runs. It seems that the Colonel, being a very wise guy, runs Mr. Silver only in enough races to have him work up through his conditions and up to the Cup races, but no more. But in seven out of every ten races he runs, he wins. So, I am thinking that maybe his jockey is pulling him in those he loses so that the odds in his favor do not get to be overly optimistic. And then I see that earlier this year one of the few races in which he runs is called the Alexandra Stakes, and he wins by five lengths. This, to me, is not such a big deal until I learn that this race, which is held at your Ascot Racecourse, is two miles and five furlongs and several more yards long. I do not know of any race that is this long in America. To win it, Mr. Silver runs the whole thing in four minutes and forty-five seconds, which is a record for the race. So I tell myself that this is one amazing horse, and if he is looking good and is not scratched from this big race, then he is the one on which we must place our bets."

"Jolly good," I exclaimed. "A million pounds placed on Mr. Silver to win would return a fortune to you. A capital idea."

I was smiling warmly at these chaps, but they looked somewhat chagrined and stared at the carpet.

"We must confess, Doc," the fellow continued, "that we, being true sportsmen, would most assuredly put all of the ducats at our disposal on this horse to win, if only it were our money. But as it is the money of the clients, and as the clients are associated with Fleagal Eagle, the lawyer, and his friends, we have somewhat chickened out and hedged out bets. We are betting across the board on Mr. Silver as we are highly certain he will be in the money, but we are not in a position to risk putting all the eggs into one basket as we are not the owners of those eggs and the owners are known to be occasionally cantankerous. So, against our noble principles, we are playing it safe. If I was you and you are not in a position to lose a copious amount of scratch, I would suggest a similar strategy."

I nodded and commended the chaps for their well-reasoned and cautious advice. We chatted for a few more minutes, and then Holmes rose and thanked them graciously for their insights and departed in the direction of our rooms. I likewise shook their hands and did not think to ask the fellow in the yellow suit his name, and to this day, do not know what it was.

Holmes disappeared into his bedroom and, to my surprise, emerged some fifteen minutes later looking not at all like a gentleman but more like a drunken groom, ill-kempt and side-whiskered, with an inflamed face and disreputable clothes.

"Merciful heavens, Holmes," I gasped, "you are a little over-the-top, are you not? Epsom Downs is hardly the place to wander around like some drunken ostler."

"Which, if I may say so," he replied, "I shall take that as your vote of confidence and be quite certain that there is no likelihood of my being identified as London's only consulting detective. I shall take my disreputable self to the stables and seek to learn whatever I am able to from the many boys and men who are sure to be working there."

He departed, and I saw nothing of him until the following morning.

Chapter Three

They're at the Post

I rose at what I thought was an early hour, only to find Holmes already in the breakfast room puffing on his pipe and surrounded by a minor explosion of racing tabloids, and daily forms. The one in his hands was being attacked by jabs from his pencil.

"Good morning, Holmes. Any intelligence from your undercover work last evening?"

He put down his paper and shook his head slowly. "It was not difficult to confirm the information given to us by our colorful American friends," he said. "The stables in which the participating horses are being kept are indeed under close guard. The track has hired over two dozen retired marines who are guarding every door around the clock. I was able to engage one of them in conversation. He was quite cooperative, having nothing else to do after sunset when guard duty is dreadfully boring. He made it quite clear that no one was permitted inside the stables except those whose names were on the lists, and they were accompanied to their specific stalls and back out again. So not much chance of any skullduggery on that front unless someone were able to bribe one of the guards."

"What about the jockeys?"

"They are all housed at the small inn some two blocks down the road. It is also guarded by marines, and again no one is allowed entry who is not on an approved list, and every jockey has a marine minding him around the clock."

"Good heavens," I said. "Why, a gathering of heads of state would not have that much protection and surveillance. The race organizers really have gone all out to make sure that this event is clean of any corruption."

"Yes," said Holmes. "There are fourteen horses in the race, which leaves me with fourteen men and their entourages to hold as possible suspects. The rewards for the winner of the race are enough to tempt anyone."

The Race of the Century, the Wheatcroft Cup, was scheduled for four o'clock in the afternoon. Over 70,000 spectators had descended on Epsom, and by noon, the racecourse grounds and the surrounding lands were a beehive of laughter and sporting games of all sorts. As the hour of the starting bell approached, the crowds moved into the stands. Holmes, courtesy of Scotland Yard, had secured for us some of the most desirable seats in the Queen's Stand, just ahead of the finish line and high enough to have a clear view of the entire course. Every seat around us was taken, mostly with very posh looking ladies and gentlemen, all dressed to the nines. The toffs, pretending to be learned sportsmen, were reciting horse race statistics to the ladies in their attempts to impress them, and the ladies were pretending to be impressed. All in all, it was a jolly pleasant afternoon.

At 3:30 pm, the horses with their owners and jockeys did their parade past. The American horses had been equipped with a blanket that bore the design of the Stars and Stripes, and the English bore the Union Jack. It did occur to me for a brief second that neither of the flags was honored by having a man bounce his gluteus maximus up and down upon it, but any such insistence on protocol was obviously not being considered this afternoon.

Every one of the horses looked magnificent. Their manes carefully tied up, their coats brushed and shining, and their jockeys resplendent in gleaming new silks. The crowd around me were all claps and cheers, and laughter as each of the horses walked past. The favorites – Lord Commodore, Vindication of Yarmouth, Paul Revere, Valentine, Epigraph, and Clam – all received warm applause and encouragement from their fans.

Then the crowd became silent, and I could hear only a few gasps of awe. Coming into view was Mr. Silver, two full hands taller than the rest of the horses, and with a massive chest and upper legs that made the others look like scrawny nags. His color was a brilliant white, such that would diminish a bride's wedding dress if seen alongside. The sunshine bounced off his back and side, rendering him almost a supernatural apparition, a ghost horse. He strutted like a stallion in command of his obedient brood of mares. His jockey, Donny Cotter, splendid in new red and black silks, lifting his helmet, smiled and waved to the stands.

The spectators were obligated to respond, and they did so with quiet, reverential applause. As the horses were led to the starting gate on the old Cup Course, we again took our seats, and the murmuring began.

Through my field glasses, I watched as Mr. Silver, bearing the number 2, was led into the number 1 post position. Coming in after him was Vindication of Yarmouth, wearing the distinguished Biggleswade colors. The horses were quiet and well-behaved, all led with no problems to the line by the starters. They did not appear to anticipate any trouble. The one horse that has caused a bit of a stir in the Derby, Rheingold of Reading, strutted calmly into place. Beside him, the repeated stakes winner and crowd favorite, Clam, came into line. The rest of the horses, the pick of the crop from both sides of the Atlantic Ocean, all took their places, spreading across the entire width of the track.

Everybody was in line. The bell sounded, the starting mesh dropped, and they were off. The line exploded forward as if shot from a row of artillery. Within a few seconds, they were all at full gallop and moving like a thundering horde. Fourteen of the world's best thoroughbreds were all straining to pull ahead of each other.

By the first half-furlong, the closely packed cluster had thinned out.

It looked like the early lead went to Paul Revere. Yes, it was Paul Revere, one position out from the rails, and going for the lead with Lord Commodore on the outside. Mr. Silver was away very well and had good position on the rail as they were moving for the first turn on the old Cup Course. Mr. Silver was moving up to join the leaders. Clam, showing the power he had used when winning the Preakness, on the outside, was also moving along strongly.

As they came through the turn, it was Clam and Mr. Silver right together. Paul Revere had third behind them, and then it was Lord Commodore, and trailing behind him was Epitaph as they approached the second turn. Those two, Clam and Mr. Silver were running together, with Clam on the outside. Clam pulled ahead, with Mr. Silver second as they came around the next turn and entered the long, punishing run up the hill.

I watch through my field glasses. Holmes was doing the same, and I could hear him muttering beneath his breath, "Come on there, boy, you can do it. Come on."

Behind us, the toffs and ladies were on their feet and starting to cheer.

The horses had reached the hill. Behind the front two, Clam and Mr. Silver, a large gap was opening up. By midway up the hill, it had extended to six lengths, then make it eight lengths back to Paul Revere and Lord Commodore, with Epitaph trailing closely. Then they were into the hill. It had become a match race now. Mr. Silver was on the inside by a head; Clam on the outside. These two magnificent animals had opened up ten lengths on Paul Revere, who was in third by a head, with Lord Commodore in fourth. Then it was another eight lengths back to Epitaph, with Bayard and Desborough and the remainder of the field bunched up well behind.

The crowd behind me were shouting instructions to the horses and jockeys oblivious to the impossibility of being heard by them.

The galloping horses continued up to the top of the hill. I could see that Mr. Silver had taken the lead. He had it now by a length and a half. Clam was still second. Ten lengths back was Paul Revere and Lord Commodore. They were approaching the turn now and nearing the descent of the hill. At they entered the turn, it was Mr. Silver. He looked like he was opening. His lead was increasing. Make it three lengths, then three and a half. He was moving toward Tattenham Corner and holding onto a large lead. Clam was in second, but then it was a long way back to Paul Revere and Lord Commodore. Into the corner, it was Mr. Silver, and he was blazing along. They passed the halfway pole with the time reading just under two minutes.

Mr. Silver was widening now. He was moving like a tremendous machine. It was Mr. Silver by twelve … then Mr. Silver by fourteen lengths on the final turn. Clam was dropping back, tiring, and it looked like Paul Revere and Lord Commodore would catch him. They were coming up to him. Clam could not keep the pace through a long cup race. But now Mr. Silver was all alone. As he began the long descent down the hill, he was a sixteenth of a mile away from the rest of the horses in a position that seemed impossible to catch.

The crowd in the Queen's Stand was on its feet, screaming. A quick glance over to the Grandstand told me that 70,000 more were shouting in ecstasy, watching history unfold in front of them.

Now Mr. Silver was into the final stretch. He was leading the field by eighteen lengths. Behind him, Lord Commodore had taken second, and Paul Revere moved into third, passing Clam. With nothing between him and the finish line, the great white colt had opened a twenty-two length lead. No horse had ever run this fast.

"He can't keep it up," cried one chap behind me. "You'll kill him, Donny," shouted another. Everyone was on their feet. Several more were shouting their fear that Mr. Silver would collapse before the final stretch.

Even Holmes was on his feet, his eyes glued to this magnificent, this massive, this supernatural white beast. Mr. Silver was going to win the Wheatcroft Cup, utterly demolishing the rest of the field. He came thundering down to the wire, an unbelievable, an amazing performance. He hit the finish, twenty-five lengths in front. Maybe more.

Lord Commodore was now approaching and would make second, with Paul Revere third, and Epitaph fourth. Clam, a superb horse but without the stamina to go the distance had faded to fifth.

We had observed an amazing, unbelievable performance by a supernatural horse. It was as if every one of us knew that we would never, if we lived to a hundred, see anything that came close to the miracle we had just witnessed.

The shouts from the crowd continued unabated. We watched as the official approached the tote board and posted the results. Mr. Silver had won by thirty-one lengths and broken the course record by more than two seconds.

All around us, men and women were embracing each other. Some ladies had fainted and were being totally ignored by the men at their sides, who were up on their chairs, stomping, and shouting.

I could not restrain myself and threw my arms around Sherlock Holmes. It mattered not that it was like hugging a gate post, he stiffened and gave me a thin smile.

"Please, Watson, get a grip on yourself. It was a horse race, not a coronation."

Eventually, the cheering subsided, and the crowds moved down towards the track, straining to see into the winner's circle. Mr. Silver, led by Colonel Ross, with Donny Cotter on his enormous back, was approaching. As he came near, the crowds became silent. Men removed their hats, which I thought a bit much until I saw that Our Gracious Sovereign Herself was on her way to the circle. The crowd parted as she entered, sitting in a push-chair and followed by several members of the Royal Family and our Prime Minister, Lord Salisbury. Behind him was Mr. Garret Hobart, the Vice-President of the United States. He was smiling graciously although I suspected that inside he was seething since, like all Americans, he detested losing, and he especially hated such an overwhelming victory by the Empire that America so relentlessly prided itself on having once defeated.

As we worked our way through the madding crowd, I knew that I was about to incur the disdain and admonishment of Sherlock Holmes when I made my confession.

"I am terribly sorry, Holmes, but I shall have to make a small detour down to the bookmakers. I have a small ticket on the winner and stand to win a little."

His reaction was not at all what I had expected.

"Do you indeed?" he smiled. "Why congratulations. Allow me to accompany you. Such an occasion of good fortune should be shared between friends."

I was shocked. Holmes utterly loathed being squeezed and bumped about by the great unwashed, but he was all smiles, and we elbowed our way to the bookie with whom I had placed my bet. In return for my £20 ticket, he peeled off my wager and another £20 in return for my bet on Mr. Silver to show. I beamed with pleasure as I stuffed the bills into my pocket.

"Quite right," I said. "Now we can visit the pub for a round and celebrate. My treat."

"Not quite yet," said Holmes. "I have a bit of a detour to make as well. Please follow me."

I started to do as he requested, and then stopped in my tracks, grabbed his arm, and turned him around to face me.

"Sherlock Holmes! I am shocked, shocked. You … you placed a bet. I cannot believe it. Now I have seen everything."

I was utterly stunned. "How much? How much did you bet?"

Holmes tried to maintain his stone face, but a wisp of a smile flickered at the corners of his mouth. He reached into his pocket and handed me his ticket.

Had my jaw not been attached to my head, it would have hit the floor.

"Merciful heavens, Holmes. You put £1000 pounds on the ghost horse to win? Have you lost your mind? What if you had lost? You would have been ruined. Holmes, I cannot believe that you did this!"

I was without words. It was beyond belief that this man who placed such unparalleled value on reason and eschewed emotion and passion at all costs would have taken such a risk.

"I believe," he said, with a touch of smugness, "that from time to time, I have said that once you have eliminated all other possibilities …"

"Good Lord, Holmes. I know what you have said. But what were you thinking? This is madness."

"As I was saying, once you have eliminated all other horses in the field, the one that remains must be the winner. A handsome bet on Mr. Silver was quite logical. Elementary, my dear Watson. However, if you are buying the round of ale, then I suppose I must cover the dinner."

I could not stop shaking my head as we walked toward the high-flyer bookmakers section, and I watched as Holmes pocketed over four thousand pounds.

The scene outside the stands was one of boisterous chaos. Hawkers and touts were everywhere, enticing anyone who was fortunate to have placed a winning bet to part with their so recently acquired wealth. Carriages and cabs were clogging up the road as throngs of Londoners made their way back to the train stations. As Holmes and I walked back to the hotel, he chatted on pleasantly, demonstrating that even the most resolute of rational men is susceptible to the euphoria that overtakes a man's mind when he finds himself holding a winning ticket.

After a round of ale, which I was honored to pay for, Holmes became somewhat more serious.

"Kindly indulge me, my dear doctor, and let us return to the Derby Arms close by the racecourse for our supper. While this past hour has been a delightful interlude of pleasant revelry, I cannot escape my responsibility to Scotland Yard, who requested my professional services. While the race itself appears to have been run without any criminal manipulation, I am still faced with the murder of the jockey. We shall not learn any more about the case by sitting here, but I expect that anyone who has any insights into the foul deed can now be found at the adjacent pub, and, with luck, his tongue may be loosened by his imbibing."

The gathering in the Derby Arms was, as expected, loud and raucous, filled with tobacco smoke, laughter, and shouting. The barmaids were moving as quickly as possible through the tightly-packed crowd of patrons, their own hands holding several mugs of ale, and struggling to keep others' hands away from their legs and buttocks. In one corner, I could see our American friends chatting with others from their homeland. Several I recognized from the parade as the owners of Clam, Paul Revere, and Epitaph. The New York brethren were buying the drinks, and I could overhear snatches of their conversation. "Yeah, the fix was in…" or "never do I know a racecourse with turns going both ways and hills…" and "you guys must demand a return match, but next time in the good old U S of A …" I nodded in their direction, and they smiled back, lifting a glass of ale as they did so.

The old chap, Lord Atherstone, was standing at the bar looking shy and confused and every so often glancing over the crowd with the look in his eye of the sly old fox that he was known to be.

The brash young Lord Biggleswade, whose horse, Lord Commodore, had been the fastest of all the English steeds, was sitting at a large table, speaking in a loud voice, mostly about himself and his horse, and was constantly groping the poor barmaids as they squeezed past him and saying appallingly rude and lascivious things to them. He had a lot of growing up to do and was a long way from acting like the gentleman he was bred to be.

Throughout the room, I repeatedly heard the name "Mr. Silver" and the endless retelling of his astounding run, each time with some additional explanation and commentary gratuitously provided by the teller. The not altogether surprising observation was the non-presence of Colonel Ross or any of his entourage. Twenty-five years ago, in Afghanistan, he had a reputation as a teetotaler and as a man of scrupulous personal discipline who would have to be in the middle of a pitched battle before breaking his routine bedtime of half-past ten o'clock.

Holmes and I spent over two hours engaging various fellows in conversation, but each time we attempted to turn the talk to the death of the jockey, we were, in a friendly way, ignored or rebuffed. The mood was too celebratory, and no one was interested in ruining the joyful conviviality by dwelling on a sad but now past event.

The eleventh hour of the evening had come and gone when Holmes gave me a tug on the arm, leaned his head toward my ear, and over the din said, "We may as well be on our way. There is nothing more to be gleaned from here. They are all becoming steadily more drunk. Let us go."

I nodded my agreement, and we started to push and elbow our way toward the door. We were within a few feet of it when it suddenly flew open violently, and a young man in a groom's outfit burst in. At the top of his lungs, he screamed,

"THE STABLES ARE ON FIRE!"

Chapter Four

They're Off

For a second or two, the entire pub became silent. Then men leaped to their feet and rushed toward the door. Holmes and I were pushed from behind and swept out into the street. En masse, the crowd began to run the short distance back to the racecourse. I am no runner, and if I were ever to doubt that fact, the pain in my leg from the Jezail bullet of so many years ago provided an irrefutable reminder. Holmes and many of the younger chaps passed me, but then we were halted by a row of trainers and track officials all shouting, "Stand back! Stand back! The men are bringing the horses out. Stand back!"

Behind them, we all watched in horror. Fire was engulfing the back section of the first stable, the one closest to the racecourse in which were kept the horses that had taken part in the Century Race. The front door of the stable was wide open, and several men were bravely running into the building and one by one leading the horses out and handing them off to other men who quickly moved them away from the growing conflagration.

A fellow came running and coughing from the burning building. I recognized him as Robert Blinden, who just two days ago had first raised our suspicions about the death of the jockey.

"We can't get the last four!" he cried. "They are going crazy. Their hooves are flying all over. We can't get close to them."

Proof of his words was given as two of his colleagues came staggering from the building with a third chap being held up between them. I ran forward to give whatever medical attention I could. As I did, I was knocked off my feet by a man running at full speed. From behind, I watched as a very tall man, carrying his suit jacket in one hand and a riding crop in the other went running past me and into what had become the gates of hell. All of us stared in silence until, a minute later, Harry-the-Horse emerged from the barn, his suit jacket was wrapped around the head of Paul Revere. The big racehorse was following him obediently. Harry was giving the beast hard whips to his neck with the crop and dragging him forward. As soon as he was a safe distance, he handed the bridle rope to another man, pulled his jacket off the horse's head, and turned back to the stable door.

"Doctor!" Robert shouted at me. "Give me your coat. Hurry!" I ripped my suit coat off and handed it to him. Other men behind me did likewise and handed their garments to two other grooms. The three of them then turned and ran back into the flaming building. The fire by now had moved up the walls and was approaching the front section. The roof in the back section was now in flames.

As a doctor in the medical corps, I had stood behind battle lines and watched as brave men charged forward to engage the enemy, knowing that they stood a very high risk of dying by doing so. Now that dreadful feeling returned, and I could sense my heart pounding and my breathing becoming fast and shallow as we waited, hoping and praying that these brave chaps would get out before the inferno collapsed on top of them or they were overcome by the smoke and heat.

One by one, they came. First, the two grooms, and then came Harry, pulling a very skittish Clam behind him.

"Is that all of them?" shouted someone in the crowd behind me.

"I'll check!" came the shout back from Robert, and he turned and ran back toward the stable door.

"No!" I screamed at him. "It is not worth it. No!"

He could not hear me and raced back in, using my suit coat as a blanket around his head to protect him from the flaming embers that were now falling from the roof and the rafters into to the interior of the barn.

"He is mad with courage," said Holmes, who was now standing beside me, his arm through mine and clasping me tightly.

Men of the racetrack are not given to sincere utterances of religious expression. But I could hear voices crying out their orisons to the Almighty on behalf of the man who had run back into the fire. Then, as the back part of the building collapsed and fell to the ground with a roar and an explosion of flame, we saw the form of a very brave man emerge from the door. He was running for his life, coughing and gasping. When he was out of the reach of the flames, he collapsed, and several men ran forward, lifted him, and pulled him back away from the fire.

Between his coughs and gasps for fresh air, Robert sputtered. "They're all out. The stalls are empty. We got them all."

A spontaneous round of *hurrahs,* and *well done* and similar accolades came from the crowd, who by now must have numbered over a hundred.

The building was beyond saving, and the firemen from the village were now present and directing streams of water on the parts of the structure nearest to the other stables to make sure that the fire could not spread. I bent down to where Robert was sitting and listened to his breathing. He was still coughing, but there was no blood in his phlegm, and the convulsions of his chest were subsiding. Holmes stood beside me, transfixed by the sight in front of us. The entire edifice was now in flames. Sections of it continued to collapse, and soon it was no more than a roaring bonfire, timbers, and straw and siding all piled up together and set to burn until it had consumed itself.

Holmes's body suddenly twisted around as a large hand pulled on his shoulder. Harry-the-Horse then grabbed my friend by his shirt front and brought Holmes's face within three inches of his own.

"Look here, Mr. Detective," Harry said in a tone that left little threat to the imagination. "You better figure out who torches this stable, and when you do, you better tell me. Because when you do, that guy is going to meet the business end of my Roscoe. You got that, Mr. Detective."

I knew that Sherlock Holmes did not take kindly to being threatened and that he was a skilled pugilist who would not back down from a fight even with a man so much larger than he as Harry-the-Horse. Instead, I watched as he raised both his hands, placed them warmly on Harry's shoulders, and spoke directly to him.

"Mr. Harold Corrigiano," said Holmes. "You have my word that I will do exactly that. You and I will be fighting for the same side. Now unhand me, sir, and compose yourself, and give me the information I need."

Harry let go of Holmes's clothing and quietly growled. "What do you need to know that is not as obvious as the snoze in the middle of your puss?"

He was still holding Holmes uncomfortably close to him. He relaxed his grip and dropped his hand. Holmes did likewise and let his hands slide off of Harry's shoulders.

"I am not," said Holmes, "questioning what you have told me, but I must know how it is that you are so certain that this was an act of arson."

"If you must know how I know, Mr. Detective, it is because I see a torch at work more than once or twice. So, I know that when a fire starts halfway down the side of a wall of a building and then within a few seconds spreads only in one direction and it is around the back of the building, and halfway up the other side then that is

47

the work of a torch and not of Mother Nature. Now I am not disputing the right of a torch to set his own building on fire in order to collect his insurance, nor to set the building of his competitor on fire in order to put him out of business for a while. But there are rules to doing so. The first is that you leave the door wide open so no one gets hurt, which this torch did. But it is solidly against the rules to do anything that will harm animals, especially magnificent racehorses, since they do not do anything ever to hurt you. In that barn, I see horses in complete fear, and terror like as no racehorse should ever have to experience, and if it is not for some brave kids who go running into the fire, then those horses would all be suffering beyond anything you or I can imagine and ending up dead. And nobody is allowed to get away with doing that. Now, do you get it, Mr. Detective?"

Holmes smiled back at Harry. "Yes, my friend, I get it, as you say. I shall make certain that whoever perpetrated this atrocity is brought to justice. You may have my word on that, sir."

Harry-the-Horse nodded and turned and walked away. Holmes and I walked back up the road to the hotel. He did not speak any more to me that night. After one more brandy and two more pipes, he retired to his room. I then did the same.

I did not sleep well, nor did Holmes. At seven o'clock the next morning, we met in our suite and descended to the breakfast room together. It was almost empty, except that in the corner, with his hands clasped together on the table in front of him, was Colonel Ross, neatly dressed and with trim side-whiskers and an eyeglass. He was looking directly at us as we entered and took our seats, whereupon he rose and walked over to our table.

"Good morning, Mr. Holmes; Doctor Watson," he said as he lowered his long, lean frame into a chair at our table. "I have been waiting for you."

"That much," said Holmes, "is quite apparent. As I am quite certain that it was not so that we could heap yet more congratulations upon you for your wonderful win yesterday, I have to assume that you have some reason to seek my services. Pray sir, allow me to pour you a cup of coffee while you state your case." He offered a cup of coffee to the Colonel as he spoke.

Colonel Ross gave a shallow nod in return. "My horse, my trainer, and one of my grooms have all disappeared."

He paused as the meaning of his words sunk in.

"I have sent word to the police, but they are entirely occupied with the events of last night. Therefore, I wish to engage your services – the price is of no matter – and I wish you to commence immediately. Please enjoy your breakfast quickly. I have already eaten."

He took a sip of his coffee, put down the cup, sat back, and folded his arms across his chest. He did not take his eyes off Holmes's face at any time.

"I accept your request," said Holmes. I was fairly certain that none but I, who have come to know him better than any other man, could detect the faint widening of his eyes and smallest trace of a smile as he spoke. "And, if you will forgive my bad manners by eating in front of you, I shall begin at once by asking you some necessary questions."

"Very good, Mr. Holmes. Proceed."

"A chronology of events would be useful. Please begin with your time in the winner's circle with your splendid horse, Mr. Silver, and your jockey, and end with your entry into this room. Please, sir, proceed."

The Colonel took another sip of coffee and then refolded his arms, leaned back, stretched his long legs under the table and began.

"My jockey, Donny Cotter, dismounted and departed to the jockeys' quarters. My trainer, John Straker, led the horse back to the stables. I walked with him, accompanied by my sister and her husband, who had been my guests at the race. We …"

"Sorry to interrupt," said Holmes. "why were you not accompanied by your wife?"

"For the simple reason, Mr. Holmes, that I do not have one. And, therefore, neither do I have any children. I spent the first forty years of my adult life married to Her Majesty's Forces, and since then to my horses. Your life, I have observed, is following a similar trajectory."

"It is indeed. Please, sir, continue."

"At the stable, the saddle and blanket and bridle were removed, and Mr. Silver was given to the grooms to hotwalk and then rub down and inspect. Nothing different from what is done after any strenuous race. I could see that all was being done decently and in order, and so I departed from Epsom on the next train and returned to London."

"You did not stay to enjoy the celebrations?"

"If you mean that I did not wish to be suffocated by the sycophantic press and a host of unknowns claiming to be my dear friends, then that is correct. I engage in horse racing for the thrill of the win, sir, not for the adulation of the masses. Besides which, the glory should be given to the rider, the trainer, and the horse. I am only an old soldier who happens to be the fortunate owner."

'Yes. I suspect that some other owners do not share your modesty, but that is another matter. Where in London did you go?"

"I bid good-bye to my sister and brother-in-law at Victoria and took a cab to my club, the United Service Club on Pall Mall. I took my supper there, read for an hour, and went to bed. The other members gave me many friendly smiles and nods, as they had heard the results of the race, but none attempted to engage me in conversation, knowing such is my disposition."

"Yes," said Holmes. "After retiring to your room, something must have happened."

"It did. The night porter knocked on my door just after midnight. News of the fire had come in with some of the late-arriving members, and a telegram had arrived for me. He thought I should see it even if it meant waking me. It was sent by my jockey. You may read it."

He handed it to Holmes, who handed it on to me. It ran:

```
Terrible fire in Epsom stable. All horses
said to be safe. Will check on Mr.
Silver. Will contact you in the morning.
Cotter.
```

"And upon receiving this? What then?" queried Holmes.

"I returned to my bed."

Holmes stared in disbelief, as did I. Colonel Ross observed our disbelief and continued.

"Gentlemen, I have been in command of other men for five decades. If you recruit excellent men, then you know that the best strategy is to leave them in charge of their duties and not interfere. I knew that I had fine men working for me and that they would do the right thing. I returned to my bed and went back to sleep."

"But you are here now. What changed?" asked Holmes.

"At four o'clock in the morning, the night porter again woke me up. When I opened the door, I saw that he was accompanied by my jockey, Donny Cotter, and ..."

"Please, sir," snapped Holmes. "How in the world did your jockey get to London? At four in the morning, there are no trains running back to London, and no cabs."

"The celebrations ended with the fire. Donny had gone up to the stables to make sure that Mr. Silver was taken care of. Jockeys do seem to develop a rather emotional attachment to their mounts. He could not find the horse nor my trainer. After an hour of frantic searching and asking around, he felt he had no choice but to inform me. The telegraph office was closed, so he came to London and to my club."

"How?"

"He is a top-ranked jockey and has learned to use his imagination. He rode a horse."

"To London?" asked Holmes, incredulously.

"Where else would he go?"

"In the middle of the night?"

"That, sir, is how the hours between midnight and four o'clock in the morning are usually described."

"He must have been galloping quickly, all the way."

"No, he had to stop several times and let the horse rest and be watered."

"Quite so. Yes, of course. I assume that you then took the early morning train back here. Correct?"

"Correct. I went first to the site of the fire and spoke to an Inspector Gregory of Scotland Yard, and some of the other men who were standing around the area. Many had remained there since the fire. I interrogated them, and they all confirmed that there had been enormous confusion and chaos as the horses were being rescued, and the grooms and trainers were running in and out of the burning building. None could positively confirm that Mr. Silver had been led out, but neither could any say for certain that he was not."

"Really, sir," said Holmes. "How can that be? A large white horse cannot be mistaken."

"I was informed that on the first group of horses, the lads were able to throw one or two blankets over their backs to protect them from the embers. My horse was not the only one with a white face or some white coloring on his legs or haunches. It is quite possible, in the heat of the struggle, that he was led out and away unnoticed. It is also possible that he was stolen away before the fire."

"The place was guarded like the Tower of London," I offered. "How could anyone get past the sentries and remove a horse?"

"The marines," explained the Colonel, "were all dismissed once the horses had been taken out to begin the Cup race. It had been reasoned, quite logically, that any harm anyone wished to do would be done before the race, not after. Guards were no longer needed."

I said no more. Holmes sat in silence for several moments and then spoke. "I make it a practice, sir, not to reach conclusions before having as much data in front of me as I can possibly assemble. However, in your case, all fingers would appear to be pointing to your trainer and the groom, who are missing along with your horse, and who, by now, could be almost anywhere in the south of the country. By tonight, they could be in Scotland or on the Continent. You appear, sir, to have trusted the wrong men and to have been robbed of a tremendously valuable asset."

Now it was the Colonel's turn to sit in silence before speaking.

"Mr. Holmes, I have been in command of hundreds of men over the course of my life. I believe I have developed a very reliable sense of which man is to be loyal and trusted, and which is not. John Straker has worked for me for at least a decade, ever since I was retired from the BEF. I can think of no occasion when his loyalty and integrity were ever in doubt. Not one. The groom, Ned Hunter, was a young lad who had been with me for only a year but reported to Straker. It is unlikely that he acted on his own, having somehow removed Straker, and it is impossible that he convinced Straker to be disloyal. In my line of work, Mr. Holmes, you learn quickly to discern who is on the up and up and who is not."

"I am sure you do, sir," returned Holmes. "In my line of work, I have learned to assume that no one is to be trusted and that every man has his price. I intend no offense in saying so, but I would not last long as a detective if I were ever to think otherwise."

53

"I take no offense, Mr. Holmes. However, I have no additional information to give you. Kindly take whatever actions you need to straight away, and find my horse. Let me know what needs you may have. Leave no stone unturned. You know where to find me."

He rose, nodded stiffly, turned, and departed.

After he was gone, Holmes turned to me. "Any thoughts, my good doctor?"

"I suppose that we should start looking for two men who have run off with a large white horse."

Holmes lit his pipe. "I suspect that your supposition is precisely where we should not start looking."

Chapter Five

Into the Backstretch

"Come, Watson," said Holmes with decision, , getting up from the table. "Time is passing. Our sources of data and information will be departing Epsom over the next few hours if they have not already gone. Come. We must speak to them while time still permits."

He was right to have been worried. For the rest of the morning, Holmes chatted with as many chaps as he could, but preparations were well underway to transport the English horses back to their home farms and stables. The American ones were all scheduled to be taken down to Portsmouth the following morning and boarded a ship back across the ocean.

Donny Cotter, the jockey who had ridden Mr. Silver to such an exceptional victory, had organized some of the jockeys and grooms to do a complete search of all of the barns and other buildings in and around the racecourse, looking for any sign of the missing horse. It was already the end of the racing season, and most of the facilities had been closed up for the winter. There was no sign of the horse, or of the two missing men.

Such additional information as we were able to obtain only confirmed and added to what we already knew. The last anyone could definitely remember seeing Mr. Silver was when his trainer, John Straker, led him back into his stall in the stable closest to the race track, the one that was now no more than a charred heap of smoldering rubble. It was being soaked with water and then lifted into trash wagons and hauled away by some local lads who had been hired for the unpleasant job.

Sadly, a pall had descended on the grounds. Few were interested in stopping their tasks and trying to remember the details of the previous night. They just wanted to finish up what needed to be done and be on their way. John Straker and Ned Hunter, the missing men, were well-known and well-liked within the tight circles of the racing fraternity. Not a man would say a word against them, and when pressed by Holmes, the men of the track just shook their heads and said, "I don't know. I just do not know."

It was even less productive the following morning. The transport wagons had come for the American horses, and attention was being given to seeing them off. Their trainers, grooms, and jockeys all bade adieu to their English counterparts, shook hands, and shouted about "Next year! See you in New York!"

At noon we had some lunch, checked out of the hotel, and took a cab over to the train station.

"If we can catch the two o'clock back to Victoria," observed Holmes, "I should be able to put the Irregulars to work before the end of the afternoon. If a large white horse has been seen in London, they will know about it."

At two o'clock, we were standing on the platform with our valises as the train pulled up. It was already crowded with those who had enjoyed one last weekend at Brighton before saying a final goodbye to the season. I was stepping into our cabin with Holmes right behind me when I heard a voice shouting. Running at full speed at the far end of the platform was a page boy.

"Mr. Holmes! Mr. Sherlock Holmes. Wait!"

He kept running and shouting while doing so. I looked at Holmes, knowing that if we stepped back away from the train, we were certain to miss it, and it would be another two hours before the next one.

He gave a look of resignation and turned around.

The boy was soon up to us. "Are you Mr. Sherlock Holmes? Are you?" he said between gasps for air.

"I am he," said Holmes, whereupon the lad handed him a note.

"It's from the inspector, sir. He said I had to stop you from getting on the train. He wants you, sir."

The note, written hastily, only said:


```
Holmes. You must return to the Downs.
Come at once. Gregson.
```


We turned around, hailed one of the few cabs that was still at the Epsom Station, and returned to the racecourse. By this time, it was almost devoid of people, and it felt a bit ghostly as we walked past the Grandstand and on to the only place where we could see any activity – the burned-out shell and ruins of the stable barn. As we neared, I could make out the tall body, lion-like hair, and beard of Inspector Gregson in his familiar trench coat, standing in the midst of the charred remains. He saw us and beckoned us toward him. A path of sorts had been cleared, and we made our way over burnt timbers, doors and sides of stalls, charred saddles and blankets, and mounds of the ashes that once had been straw.

Gregson was standing where the door to one of the stalls would have stood. In front of him, inside what had been a stall, there was a large tarpaulin on the floor. I did not have to ask what was underneath it. I knew the smell immediately. The last time I had near gagged on it was at the disastrous Battle of Maiwand twenty years ago. It was the stench of burnt flesh.

Gregson said nothing. He nodded to two of the workers, and they pulled back the tarpaulin. Lying in the stall was the body of a massive horse. The entire exposed side of the beast was blackened. In many places, the hide had been burned right off, and the flesh, burned to a crisp and covered with straw ash, was exposed. In the corner of the stall was a smaller carcass, a dog of the size and shape of a German Shepherd was curled up and likewise burned beyond recognition.

Lying on each side of the horse was a human body. They were on their backs, and their faces were burned beyond all recognition, as was their clothing, their torsos, and the fronts of their legs. They were also covered with ash. There was no need for questions. We were looking at the bodies of Mr. Silver, John Straker, and Ned Turner.

Gregson spoke to Holmes. "As soon as we saw what was here, I told them not to disturb anything. You are much better at this than I am, Holmes. So, I sent for you straight away. Glad the lad caught you in time. I could use your help."

For the next hour, Holmes and I examined the burnt carcasses and the remains of the stall. Holmes carefully lifted up one of the legs of the horse, revealing on the protected underside a hide of white, unscorched by the fire. Carefully we carried out the unpleasant but necessary task of examining the bodies of the two men and the dog. The Inspector kept the curious at bay but called two of them to confirm that the uncharred clothing on the backsides of the bodies was what John Straker and Ned Hunter had been wearing when last seen around the track.

When we had completed our task, Holmes rose, put his glass back in his pocket and spoke to Inspector Gregson.

"I must assume, Inspector, that you would not have sent for me so urgently if you believed that the deaths of these two men and the horse were only a tragic incident. Am I correct in that assumption, sir?"

"And I assume, Mr. Holmes," returned Gregory, "that you would not have spent the past hour on such a nasty business if *you* thought it was no more than a terrible death in a fire. Am I right, sir?"

"You are, Inspector."

"I have no theory," carried on the inspector, "about what has taken place. But the death of Leggatt, the fire after the race, and now this. It just does not smell right, if you know what I mean, Mr. Holmes?"

"I do. What report are you going to give?"

Gregory said nothing for a moment, and then, "I believe, sir, that I will tell the press of the heroic deaths of two brave men and a courageous dog who gave their lives trying to rescue the greatest racehorse of our time."

"An excellent plan," said Holmes. "And your report to Inspector Lestrade? What of that?"

"I shall tell him that there appears to have been multiple murders and that I have hired Sherlock Holmes to assist the Yard in the investigation. You know, Lestrade, Mr. Holmes. I am quite sure he will agree. And may I assume that you will as well?"

"You may."

We bid farewell to Inspector Gregory and began to walk back to the station. Holmes was walking quickly with a faintly disguised spring in his step. He was rubbing his hands together as we made our way.

"Good heavens, Holmes. At least try not to act so positively gleeful. And, confound it, stop rubbing your hands together like a giddy schoolboy."

Holmes stopped walking and looked at me. "Awfully sorry, my friend. I force myself to rub my hands for fear of starting to clap them. It is terribly unseemly of me, I do confess. I shall do my best to refrain. You might assist me in doing so by informing me of whatever observations and deductions you made based on your examinations."

I knew this question was coming. It invariably did, and just as invariably, I ended up feeling like a child at the feet of his pedagogue. I would, one more time, give it my best.

"Very well, Holmes. I did notice that both men had lumps on the back of their heads. That could have happened when they fell but more likely from having been hit. Possibly by a blackjack, or Penang-lawyer, or some such instrument."

"Excellent, Watson. And what else?"

"The entire situation looks far too neat and orderly. The clothing on the fronts of their bodies was burned off, but on their backs, it was still rather well arranged. Their shirts were still tucked into their trousers. Not at all disheveled, such as one would expect when wrestling with a violent horse."

"Exactly, and what else?"

"I really cannot go any further without reading an autopsy from the morgue. So go ahead, Holmes, and tell me what I have missed."

"You have done not badly, my friend. Solidly, not bad. Now, what about the horse?"

"What about the horse?"

Holmes smiled his condescending smile. "Mr. Silver had been tethered only by a neck rope. On sensing the fire, what would he, or any horse begin to do?"

"Buck and pull in a panic against the rope," I said.

"Precisely, and what effect would that have on the knots at either end of the tether?"

"I am sure it would pull them exceptionally tight; impossible to loosen."

"And were they?"

"I did not think to look, but I assume from your question that they were not."

"Precisely. The burnt end of the neck rope was still present and clearly loosely tied. The part that had lain under the horse's neck, and thus protected, I was able to undo easily with my fingers. Mr. Silver, powerful and enormous beast that he was, did not struggle against his fate in the least. He was dead and lying down in the stall well before the start of the fire.

"And the dog? Anything odd about finding him there?" he continued his inquisition.

"Very curious indeed. Dogs usually have more sense than to stand around and let themselves die in a fire."

"Precisely. Very odd indeed. The animal may be man's best friend, but they have their limit, and suicide on behalf of those who are not their masters is normally beyond it. In a matter of seconds, this one could have sprinted out the door to safety. He had an unchewed piece of meat in his mouth, a bribe to silence him that one that he would have been wise not to accept.".

"But then why did Robert not see them all? He said he checked every stall."

"Excellent question. Even with flames surging around you, it is impossible not to see the bodies of a very large white horse and two men lying on the ground. The answer was obvious, had you only observed and not merely looked at what was lying on top of the bodies."

"I saw," I said, now feeling defensive in a familiar way, "that they were covered with ash, pieces of burnt straw, bits of charcoal and such. The entire place was covered in the same way."

"No, my friend," Holmes rebuked me. "It was not. There was a water trough at the back of the stall, the layer of detritus was much lighter than on top of the bodies. Someone had piled a layer of straw on top of them, sufficient that they could not be seen and appearing like no more than fallen bales to someone looking in quickly. And one more thing, Watson. What did you smell?"

"The entire ruined structure smelled of fire and the stall of charred flesh. What else might I have smelt?"

"The earth under it all had a faint scent of kerosene or coal oil or other such fuel. It was noticeable most on the places that had not been underneath the bodies, and less so on those places that were."

"Ah ha," I said. "So somebody, likely more than one, drugged the horse and the dog, knocked the men out with a blackjack, piled straw on top of them so they could not be seen, soaked the stall with kerosene, then poured more fuel around the walls of the building, and lit it on fire. Is that it?"

"Yes, my friend, that is it."

By this time, we had reached the train station and were standing on the platform, waiting for the late afternoon express to Victoria. I asked what, to me, was another obvious question.

"Please, Holmes. If a jockey, a trainer, a groom, and the prize racehorse to which they were associated are all the victims of foul play here in Epsom, why are we returning to London?"

"It is elementary, Watson. A murderer must have a motive for murder, an opportunity to carry it out, and access to the means for doing so. We already know how, when and where the killings took place. What we do not know is *why*. The answer to that question does not lie in the ruins of a stable at a racetrack. It may lie in London, or in America, or elsewhere. And that, my friend, is why we are leaving Sussex."

During the one-hour trip back to London, Holmes said nothing. He sat with his hat pulled down on his forehead, his hands in front of his chest, with his fingertips all touching each other, and his eyes closed. From time to time, I noticed his lips move as he carried on a debate inside his most peculiar brain.

The next day's newspapers were filled with the story. Ned Hunter and John Straker were hailed as martyrs who had valiantly given their lives while attempting to save the greatest racehorse in the world. Then came the hagiographic accounts of the horse. The great silver beast, the supernatural offspring of the mysterious white horses of Wiltshire, had run like no mortal horse had ever run. Never had there been a race like the Race of the Century at Epsom Downs, and never would there be again.

Our Gracious Queen issued a statement expressing her deep sorrow and praising the ultimate sacrifice the brave men had made for such a noble cause. A telegram had arrived from Mr. William McKinley, the President of the United States of America, expressing his condolences, assuring the public that his thoughts and prayers were with the families of the men, and praising their courage.

Poor Robert Blinder did not come off so well. The chap who had risked his life to run back into the burning building became the object of ridicule. How could he have not seen the prostrate bodies of a huge horse and two men? Did he really check on every stall? Or had he merely run inside the door, waited for his moment of glory, and run back out again? "Blind Bobby Blinden" was scorned by many of the lower-class newspapers, and even *The Times* questioned why his report was believed, as it was well-known that he was not exactly an intellectual giant.

Chapter Six

Up the Hill

Two days later, I received a note from Holmes asking if I might join him for tea as soon as my patients were through for the day. I happily complied, and hurried off to 221B Baker Street, anxious to learn what progress he had made. He greeted me warmly and asked, courteously as always, if I might join him on an excursion that evening and another one the following morning. Having sent word to my dear wife that I had expected such a request, I immediately agreed.

Notwithstanding my eagerness to join in the quest, I demanded to know what it was that we were going to be up to.

"You will recall, I am sure, the rules of arson as quoted to us by Mr. Corrigiano on the night of the fire with respect to whose property it was reasonable to burn down."

"If my memory serves me," I replied, "Harry said that you could torch your own property in order to collect the insurance, or that of a competitor so as to gain an economic advantage over him. Something along those lines, was it not?"

"Precisely," said Holmes. "He might have added the ancient motive of revenge, or the unarguable truth, even if spoken by the French, of *cherchez la femme*. However, neither of these latter two appear to have any purchase in this case. Therefore, we must ask, in keeping with the insight of Harry-the-Horse, *cui bono?* Who might benefit from collecting what is most likely a considerable insurance claim, and which competitor might now be enriched by these tragic events?"

I pondered his comment. "I suppose that the Epsom Downs Racecourse Company will lay a claim to replace the stable barn, but it was a rather new structure and highly regarded. It does not make much sense to burn down a perfectly good building that is helping you earn your quite considerable profits."

"Agreed," said Holmes. "Pray continue."

"That would leave the owner, Colonel Ross, and honestly Holmes, I cannot imagine that he would stoop to such a despicable level of crime. And it would make no sense for him to hire you." ,

"Fortunately," Holmes responded, a bit haughtily, "my imagination is not so delicately constrained as yours. I have been hired before merely for pretense and appearances. It may well be that he is a possibility that we will eliminate early on, but until that time, he remains suspect, and we must pay him a visit."

"You cannot have asked me over at this time of day with the intent of now traveling to Wiltshire," said I.

"Of course not, this evening we shall begin our investigations with other competitors who stood to profit. Lord Biggleswade the younger, and Lord Atherstone, the not young, are also on my list."

"But their estates are miles from London."

"Well then, we shall just have to begin with those who have conveniently remained in our fair city. My Irregulars have informed me that our American friends are still around and lodged over in Bloomsbury. They stand to benefit, I dare say more than somewhat, by the demise of the winning horse. Therefore, they remain on my list of suspects, howbeit not near the top."

"Heavens, Holmes. That Harry fellow was terribly upset by the fire. Surely you do not suspect that he was merely acting?"

"You must not forget, my dear Watson, that he is an American of Italian lineage and therefore highly capable of dramatized emotional displays. So, Watson, are you up for a visit? It is close enough for a pleasant walk on a lovely autumn evening. Our New Yorkers are guests at the Hotel Russell."

In a brisk half-hour, we had made our way through Marylebone and into Bloomsbury. The newly opened Hotel Russell had been hailed as a monument to architectural genius and was being compared to Kensington and Buckingham Palaces, which was a silly exaggeration. For my taste, it was an exercise in inexcusable busyness. I did concede that the dining room was splendid and the guest rooms, each with their own private water closets, were a civilized advance on any other hotel in London.

On reaching the steps of the Hotel Russell, we shooed away several stray cats and made our way up and into the lobby, and then up, and up again to the bar where, we were told by the front desk, the Americans could be found. There, at a table in the corner, sat Harry-the-Horse, a large bottle of Jack Daniels, two-thirds depleted, adjacent to his elbow.

"Ah, hello there, Mr. Corrigiano," said Holmes. "I see you are still in London."

Harry raised his head and looked at us. His eyes were reddened and not entirely clear.

"Now that is the stupidest dumb chump obvious thing that has been said to me all day, Mr. Detective. Does it look as if I am not here? Hello, Doc. Sit down and have a drink. I am more than somewhat drunk and well on my way to becoming even drunker than I am."

"Your colleagues," I observed, "Will they be joining you?"

"They are making a necessary visit to another location, to a place called Birtwick, which is in a place called Suffolk. Sorrowful's kid has demanded this of him so that he might return with a picture or other acceptable souvenir of this place for it is near and dear to the heart of his kid."

Holmes looked quite perplexed at this news, which was not surprising as there is no such place in Suffolk by the name of Birtwick. He was clearly not aware that it had been the home of Black Beauty and was, therefore, beloved of millions of girls in their early teens throughout the world.

"I fear that your friends will be disappointed," I said. "The place they have gone to visit is only an imaginary place in a work of fiction, a story told by a horse."

Harry looked at me, not so far inebriated that he was incapable of regarding me with utter disdain.

"One would think that a doctor should know that fiction is not untrue if in your head and your heart you believe it to be true. The kid believes this, and so for her, it is true, and so Sorrowful has no choice but to go and find a place that he believes to be where he is seeking."

I could not argue with such reason. In a friendly way, I noted, "It is a shame that you were not able to accompany them."

He looked as if he were about to say something when his lips began to tremble. Tears appeared in his eyes, and he dropped his face into his hands. His body was convulsing with sobs, and whimpering sounds almost like a baby were coming from his hidden face.

"My dear man," I said, ever the doctor trying to console, "my dear man. Please, sir. What is it?"

Through his sobs, he managed to say, "I could-a saved them. I could-a saved them. I could-a saved those two guys and that beautiful horse. I could-a gone back into that barn myself instead of that dopey stable boy. I would-a seen them. I could-a got them out. I could-a had class."

I placed my hand on his shoulder and said, "Looking back, we all could have done more than we did. It is always that way, Harry. You were incredibly brave, and you did everything you thought you had to do at the time."

"Thanks, Doc. Thanks. I know you are trying to be kind. But I should-a known. Those guys and that horse would be alive now if I had only done what I should-a done."

"No, Mr. Corrigiano," said Holmes sharply. "That is nonsense. They were dead before the fire started. There was nothing you or anyone could have done."

Harry lifted his head out of his hands and stared hard at Holmes. He stood and before turning away from us, said quietly but forcefully. "Do not go away. I will be back. You better still be here."

He departed in the direction of the gentlemen's room. As he passed the bar, he barked over at the barkeeper, "I need some coffee. And make it snappy."

Some five minutes later, he re-emerged, his face dripping with water. A cup of hot coffee was waiting for him. He took several slow sips on it, giving his head some vigorous shakes in between. He lit a cigarette and then spoke to Holmes.

"You are saying something, Mr. Detective, that is upsetting to my system. So maybe you better explain yourself to me more than somewhat completely else I will continue to very upset, and possibly at you."

Patiently but thoroughly, Holmes presented the evidence he had gleaned so far and the deductions that led to his conclusions.

"And so who is it," asked Harry, 'that you are thinking might have done these terrible things, for what you are saying they did is among all the deeds known to guys upon this earth, very terrible indeed."

"Anyone," said Holmes, "who stood to benefit from what has happened. And that, sir, would include the owners of the American horses as well as their agents. With the best racehorse in the world out of the running, then your horses would stand a much better chance of winning next year."

He stopped and paused and waited for a reaction.

I saw first a flash of anger pass across Harry's face, but then it was replaced by his pursing his lips and nodding slowly.

"Under normal circumstances, I should feel insulted by what you have just said, but as you are a detective and, therefore, suspicious of everyone, I will take no offense. However, you are again proving to be a dumb chump when it comes to horse races."

He turned briefly to me. "Doc, would you please illuminate your friend as to the biological fact that a horse, or a guy or a doll, or anything that lives and moves and crawls upon the face of this earth can only be five years old once in its life. A special cup race for five-year-olds cannot be participated in for two consecutive years by the same horse. Are you with me so far, Mr. Holmes?"

Holmes nodded.

"So that rules out any gain in this race should it ever take place again. Now, you are thinking that these American horses will move up in rank upon return to the United States because the number one horse is burnt to a crisp and be able to race in richer races. That again does not happen. Precisely because they have already won many stakes races is the reason they were brought over to this big race. They are now far more valuable for breeding than for running more races because every winner makes for a good stud. It is the losers who are kept racing until they fall over as long as they are even a little bit profitable. The winners, because they are now highly valuable, are also insured for a much higher amount, and so it is very important to the insurance companies that they no longer be allowed to run in races where they might hurt themselves and have to be put down and become a burden to the insurers.

"All of this is to inform you, Mr. Detective, that there is no opportunity for a reasonable return on your investment by cooking your competition, especially considering the risk to your neck by doing so. Do I make myself clear, sir?"

"You do."

"Now, as for me and my colleagues, we acknowledge, with some pride, that we are handicappers and gamblers, and from time to time, we may appear to be in a minor conflict with our colleagues in law enforcement on account of because of our gambling practices. We may, from time to time, engage in some fisticuffs when it is necessary to remind a guy that he needs to improve his behavior. However, we do not kill people like jockeys, and trainers, and grooms who have never done us any harm, and we most certainly would ourselves risk our lives if called upon to defend the life of an exceptionally great racehorse, as was most certainly your Mr. Silver."

Holmes smiled across the table. "You have helped greatly, sir. I do thank you for your time." He started to rise from his chair.

"One more thing," said Harry, "before you go. If and when you do apprehend the perpetrators of these evil deeds, which I expect you will as that is what a detective does, and if you find that such person or persons are living in the United States of America, then I am expecting that you will inform me and my colleagues of same. We will, most likely, make an exception to what I have said as to how we deal with such a guy or guys. Are you understanding me, sir?"

"I am," said Holmes.

We hailed a cab and returned to Baker Street. As we approached Holmes's abode, he observed, "This man made rather good logical sense. I believe I am safe for the time being in removing Americans from the list and concentrating on our home-grown villains. It appears that I also should learn more about horse racing."

"I would say that you are right on both counts. And shall I see you back here first thing in the morning?"

"It would be more efficient use of our time if we met at Paddington. Kindly consult your Bradshaw's and meet me in time for the first train towards Salisbury."

First thing the next morning, I bade my dear wife goodbye for the day and walked smartly over to the train station. The LSWR ran trains regularly from Paddington to the south and west, and I booked a cabin for the two-hour run. Holmes was waiting for me on the platform.

We had a corner in a Pullman and ensconced ourselves comfortably. Holmes had obtained, as he often did, several newspapers from the newsagents at the station. I spotted a copy of *Sporting News* in the bundle but resisted the temptation to make any comment. He delved into his reading materials, pencil and notebook in hand until we had passed Reading and were almost at Newbury, at which time he laid down the papers and asked me an odd question.

"My dear doctor, I am once again in need of your assistance. This sport of kings, as its subjects insist on referring to it, has a vocabulary all its own. Pray tell, what is the meaning of *a nerved horse, a pinhooker, an impost, a blanket finish, an underlay,* and *a bar-shoe?*"

I explained these and other esoteric terms to him, for which he thanked me. Then he posed another question.

"Mr. Corrigiano mentioned insurance on racehorses. Is that a common practice?"

"It is common if you have a good horse. Both Lloyds and Royal and Sun offer policies. By the time a horse wins a cup race, it has considerable value not only for future purses but more so for stud fees. I am quite certain that every horse in the Century Race was well-insured."

"Interesting. Thank you, doctor." He returned to his papers and notes and said no more until we arrived at the station in Westbury.

"I presume," I inquired, "that Colonel Ross is expecting us at King's Pyland?"

"No. On the contrary, he is expecting that he will not be seeing me again. I had a note from him advising me that since his horse had now been found, he would no longer require my services in locating the beast, and that payment of my fees and expenses would be issued promptly."

"Very well then, Holmes. On what grounds are you now going to demand an audience with him?"

"That my services have now been engaged by Scotland Yard and that he must submit himself to my questioning him if he wishes his name to be removed from the list of suspects in the murder of his trainer and groom, and possibly the earlier death of the jockey."

"Does he know that foul play is suspected?"

"Of course not. That would never do."

Chapter Seven

Around Tattenham Corner

From the station at Westbury, , we took a landau through the village and a short distance north along the Trowbridge Road toward Heyworth. On the side of a hill in the distance, I could clearly see the Great White Horse of Westbury, the massive figure created in chalk stones that was said to have been there for a thousand years and put in place to commemorate some victory of King Alfred. Scholars were not too sure on that part, but the townsfolk were quite proud of it and had planned to have it illuminated on New Year's Day to mark the beginning of the twentieth century. The local Gypsies had long considered it to have connections to the spirit world and had, as I have noted earlier, ascribed to it the siring of the now-departed Mr. Silver.

We turned into the King's Pyland Estate, and I noted that, while neat and well kept, the gate, roads, bridges, and fencing were not extravagant. To the left, there was a large stable barn and adjacent to it a full racecourse, where I observed at least a dozen horses being trained. On the right, where the grounds were more rugged, dotted with junipers and furse-bushes, I spotted several jumpers and their riders running what must have been a steeplechase course. It was not surprising that a champion racehorse had emerged from this establishment.

73

The manor house was old and simple in design, with pleasant gardens and plantings but no statuary, fountains, or such as was common in estates closer to London. All of the staff wore matching uniforms, and when moving from place to place, they were all either walking quickly or running. From what I knew of Colonel Ross, none of this was surprising.

Holmes gave his card to the chap at the door, and then we stood and waited for upwards of ten minutes before Colonel Ross appeared. He did not seem at all pleased to see us.

"Did you not receive my note, Mr. Holmes?" he snapped. "Payment of your full fee and expenses and then some has been passed on to my accountant. There is no reason for you to have come here. I am frightfully busy, and this intrusion is neither necessary nor welcome."

He might have said more and told us to be off, but Holmes raised his hand and interrupted him.

"It matters not how busy you are, Colonel. I am fully aware that I am no longer under contract to you, but I am now performing services for Scotland Yard, and you will please accommodate this intrusion and provide me with the information I request."

Colonel Ross visibly stiffened. The words "Scotland Yard" had their expected impact. It was no doubt obvious to him that criminal activity was suspected. He looked straight at Holmes and spoke brusquely.

"Very well, Mr. Holmes. Get on with your questions, Scotland Yard or not, I do not have all day."

He did not invite us into the house nor even to be seated and was not conveying any sense of good humor. Holmes proceeded to carry out a thorough howbeit respectful inquisition concerning the Colonel's actions and that of his staff during the time leading up to the fire. Colonel Ross answered the questions precisely, with an economy of words. Holmes even asked some quite pointed questions concerning the Colonel's leadership during wartime. I did not see the purpose of these, and neither, it was apparent, did the Colonel.

"Kindly inform me, Colonel Ross," said Holmes. "How many men died while under your command?"

Ross glowered back. "Three hundred and thirty-seven. And it is a matter of public record, Mr. Holmes. You could look it up and do not need me to inform you."

Holmes continued impassively. "And how many were seriously wounded and to this day are not capable of gainful employment? I suppose that it is also a matter of public record."

"It is. And the answer is six hundred and forty-two."

I noticed a reddish glow appearing in the Colonel's cheeks.

"Indeed," said Holmes, with feigned incredulity. "That is quite a number, but then, of course, they were mostly men in the lower ranks and expendable in the service of Her Majesty."

I was stunned. That was an inexcusable insult to the honor of an exemplary officer. It occurred to me that Holmes was deliberately trying to provoke the Colonel, knowing that when men are angry, they are likely to say more than they should.

Holmes continued. "Is it true that your horse was heavily insured, Colonel? I do believe it was. What was the amount of the policy?"

Colonel Ross was not, as they say, born yesterday, and he relaxed his face and body, leading me to believe that he knew exactly what Holmes was doing and why, and had no plan whatsoever of losing his temper and composure.

"Ten thousand pounds. And in case you forget to ask, I will further inform you that it was to be increased by an additional ten thousand if Mr. Silver were to win the Century Race."

"That is an enormous sum, is it not, Colonel?"

"It is. The horse was recognized to be an exceptionally valuable property."

At this point, the Colonel lost his patience with Holmes's thinly veiled accusations.

"Your time is up, Mr. Holmes. If you wish to lodge an accusation against me, then stop this pretense and do so, and I will move vigorously to have it squashed. Now, either get to your point or leave."

Holmes nodded respectfully. "Allow me, Colonel Ross, to inform you of the reasons for my having concluded that the tragic events were not an accident but a heinous criminal act."

"Very well. Speak."

Holmes succinctly explained the evidence and his deductions. Colonel Ross listened, with an occasional nod, but no other sign of emotion. When Holmes reached the end of his account, he made a plea to the Colonel.

"I would hope, Colonel, that you would be eager to assist Scotland Yard and me in apprehending whoever committed these foul deeds."

The Colonel said nothing, looking up to the hills in the direction of the great White Horse as if invoking some sort of divine equine guidance.

"You have raised some very serious concerns, Mr. Holmes, and I will grant that the evidence you have provided is persuasive. However, I will not offer any further cooperation. It is up to you to sort this entire affair out and apprehend any criminals who bring them to stand in a courtroom."

Holmes looked honestly perplexed by this reply. "I fail to understand your position, sir."

"Already, my local Gypsies are reporting glimpses of a ghostly silver horse galloping in the moonlight on the plains beneath his sire. I am told that a song has been composed. I do not object to the honor and glory this brings to the memory of such a magnificent horse. Already, Ned Hunter and John Straker are being hailed as men of courage beyond all imagining, who paid the supreme sacrifice, laying down their lives for one of God's beautiful creatures. I do not object to their being so honored. If it is now rumored about that they were merely drugged or banged on the head and murdered, their stories would be sadly diminished. When you have proof of what you have told me, that is the time that those tales of bravery and courage can be dismissed. Until that time, they were my men who died on my watch, and I am happy that they are being thought of by one and all as heroes. I doubt that makes any sense to you, Mr. Holmes, and quite frankly, I do not care. I bid you wisdom from the good Lord, and wish you a pleasant day."

He turned to go back inside his home.

We rode in silence back to Paddington. Before parting, Holmes said, "I hesitate to ask you to accompany me on a visit to another one of the suspects on my list. All I can promise is that the next fellow is more convivial even is less honorable. Might you be available on Friday to come with me to the Cotswolds?"

"I shall always be pleased to accompany you, Holmes. I must warn you that I am developing some theories of my own."

I smiled, as did he in return.

On the Friday, having assigned my patients to my neighboring doctor, I was up and off to meet Holmes again at Paddington. This time, we boarded a train for Moreton-in-Marsh by way of Oxford.

"The estate and farms of Lord Biggleswade," explained Holmes, "are just north of Stow-on-the-Wold. We should be there by eleven o'clock. I notified the younger Biggleswade of our visit, suggesting that we could arrive at nine o'clock, but he wrote back agreeing only to meet at a later hour."

"Like a diligent member of the landed gentry," I suggested, "he is most likely up early and having to look after the affairs of the estate first thing each morning."

"Although it may be mean-spirited on me," countered Holmes, "I am inclined to think that he is not up at all in the morning and only fit for company at the hour he suggested. Ah, but we shall leave that thought to be confirmed."

There are many parts of our green and pleasant land that are irenic to pass through, but none, in my opinion, to match the Cotswolds. The neat and prosperous small farms, the gentle hills interspersed with woodlots, fields bronze-colored from the fading ferns, and lovely homes still roofed with thatch that was laid two centuries ago, all conspire to bring a sense of peace to the soul. How very incongruous, I thought, that we should be traversing the district while on the hunt for a hideous and vile murderer.

Lord Biggleswade's son, Julian, had something of a reputation in London for his sense of style, compared invariably, though not always favorably, to Beau Brummell. He was a member of Boodle's on St. James, where he was reputed to engage in outrageous bets for no other reason than to demonstrate the inconsequence of his considerable riches. He appeared regularly in the back pages of the gossip press, having been seen with first one and then another socialite, most of whom were not married.

The gates of his estate were newly constructed and bounded by two massive lions that I thought were somewhat larger than those at the foot of Lord Nelson. A gleaming brass plate on the south pedestal bore the name of *Mapleton*. The gates were closed, but a young woman, dressed in a smart riding jacket, was waiting for us and opened the gate, giving us a gleaming smile of perfect white teeth as she did so. Her face said that she was no more than twenty years old and, while not particularly aristocratic in its features, was highly attractive. As she walked in front of us, I could not refrain from noting that her jodhpurs could have been painted on with a whitewash brush and left very little to the imagination.

"Good morning, Mr. Holmes and Dr. Watson, and welcome to Mapleton. We are all looking forward to your visit. You have many fans and devoted readers of your stories. I do hope that you will have a few minutes to chat with some of the staff before leaving." She added an adoring and imploring look as she uttered her kind words.

Holmes merely smiled and exchanged a meaningless pleasantry.

The long drive from the gate to the manor house was a curious experience. The drive itself, wending its way up a long hill, was fully paved with smooth brickwork. The verges were lined with magnificent gardens and at least a dozen statues on each side, all of some Greek or Roman god or goddess, and all in various stages of undress. I observed three long stable barns, all newly constructed and gleaming with a recent coat of white paint. The staff, from the gardeners through the grooms and the doorman, were all dressed in well-tailored black uniforms, accented with gold buttons and trim, and all rather physically attractive. The view from the front of the house was magnificent, such as one might have found a century ago, designed by Capability Brown.

"Quite the place, I must say," I whispered to Holmes.

"Quite the expense," he muttered back, "and with not a soul in sight over twenty-five years of age."

As we arrived at the door, Baron Julian, Lord Biggleswade the younger, bounded out of the door and cantered up to our carriage before we could descend from it. He was very stylishly dressed in a gray morning coat, with freshly pressed trousers, a royal blue cravat, accented with a large pearl stickpin. He was quite a handsome man, around his mid-thirties, I would have said, with an excellent head of curly black hair, bright blue eyes, and an athletic figure, although on the short side in stature.

"Mr. Sherlock Holmes and Doctor Watson, such a delight to have you to visit us. I do hope your journey has not been tiring. May I offer you some refreshment? No? Very well. Forgive me for being a bit on the proud side of what we have done here at Mapleton, but before we get down to anything as boring as business, I insist on giving you a tour. My excellent staff have done wonders, and it would be a treat for them, beyond anything I could ever give them, to know

79

that their efforts were seen and admired by England's most famous detective."

I was quite sure that Holmes was waiting only for the fellow to pause for breath to respond with a polite declining of the offer. He did not get the chance. The Baron did not stop his monolog.

"I have asked our lovely Edith here to give you a guided tour and answer any of your questions. Please indulge yourselves. I will be eagerly waiting to speak to you when you return. Now off you go, and enjoy." He gave us a short wave, turned his back, and went into the house.

Miss Edith was a beautiful dark-skinned young woman, a Tamil I guessed, with beautiful features and a stunning white smile. She was also dressed in a shapely riding jacket and white jodhpurs.

"Good morning, gentlemen. I am honored to be assigned this very important task. How pleasant ..."

She gave instructions to the driver to start down on of the lanes toward the large pond and, for the next hour, did not let up with her perfectly delivered explanation of things historical, botanical, geological, topographical, artistic, and spiritual. We stopped at the barns, beside which was a full training course for the thoroughbreds, and she called to a young man who appeared to be waiting for us.

"Oh, do let me introduce you, Dr. Watson and Mr. Holmes. This is Howard, our assistant trainer. Our senior trainer, Mr. Silas Brown, is not available this morning and so Howard is going to lead you through our barns. Of course, I must warn you, he is somewhat inclined to be proud if indeed a little boastful since he knows he has the finest stable of thoroughbreds in all of England. Is that not right, Howard?"

The fellow gave a laugh that fell short of spontaneous and, not allowing for a word from Holmes or me, picked up the patter and began the tour of the stables. I was feeling quite annoyed with what was clearly a staged plot to distract us from our mission, and I was sure that Holmes would be similarly displeased. To my surprise, he appeared to be quite enjoying the exercise, with a contented smile on his face. I was momentarily perplexed until I placed that same smile in my memory. I had seen it recently when we attended a performance of *Macbeth* at the Lyceum with Henry Irving strutting and fretting his hour upon the stage. There was never a moment when the audience did not know what was going to happen next, and the joy came in admiring the brilliance of the production and the excellent quality of the acting. His smile while admiring the play was the same as I now observed.

"We really mustn't be boastful..." Howard was saying as we stopped at yet another still that was festooned with ribbons, "but this season, our thoroughbreds placed in the money in over one hundred stakes and cup races. And over half of our maidens, mostly from the Sonomy stock, passed their conditions by winning on their first race. Of course, the Baron will not let us race a maiden horse unless we are quite certain he is going to do well."

We kept up the very knowledgeable tour until we had completed strolling through all of the three large barns, giving friendly greetings to numerous young staff as we did so. As we returned to the carriage, I looked over to another much smaller stable barn. Howard noticed my glance and explained. "Oh, that sir, is where we keep our stallions. For the safety of our guests, and most of our staff I have to add, we do not include it on our tours. Stallions, as I am sure you know, can be unpredictable and very likely to become agitated when visitors appear. But I assure you, gentlemen, they are the stiff backbone of our breeding program. They look after all of our breeding mares. They certainly earn their keep, sir."

Holmes nodded sagely and made yet another meaningless pleasantry.

It was close to noon when the tour ended, and we were returned to the manor house. It was a splendid warm fall day, and a lunch had been laid out on the covered porch. The silverware was glistening in the sun, and four staff, all dressed in the Mapleton uniform, were standing at ease, their backs up against the wall of the house. One of them, a good-looking young blond-haired chap, came forward and gestured for us to be seated. Again, Holmes nodded with an approving smile. He leaned toward my ear and whispered, "Our host will now appear on the count of three with apologies and a bottle of champagne. A very fine one, I assure you."

Holmes was wrong. I counted off seven full seconds before Baron Julian emerged, walking quickly, followed by a beautiful dark-skinned young woman, attired like the others in a fitted black riding jacket and tight jodhpurs. She was bearing a silver tray, upon which was a bottle of Champagne and several tall flutes.

"Gentlemen, please, a round to celebrate the morning. Splendid day is it not? I do hope you have enjoyed your brief tour. Did my wonderful young help show off my stable of past and future cup winners? I do try to get them to be a bit more modest, but what can one do? They are all so awfully proud of our champions. Ah, but enough about me and Mapleton. I must try to be a gracious host and hear from my guests. Tell me about yourselves. What did you think about your tour and our magnificent herd? Please do tell."

He paused for a moment, but not long enough for either Holmes or I to collect our thoughts and offer something to the conversation.

"No reflections?" he asked. "No deductions. Ah, well, then. A toast. To the sport of kings and to the youth of the Empire who are carrying on its great racing traditions."

"He raised his glass and then took a significant gulp.

"And, I must not be remiss," he continued. "To the Queen. Wasn't it wonderful that the old girl herself came to the race? Indeed, it was. To the Queen."

He rose as he proposed the toast, leaving Holmes and I no alternative but to rise as well.

"Now, my friends," he said, smiling broadly. "Best we get down to business. My time is terribly short, as I am sure yours is as well. Your wire to me, Mr. Holmes, said that you had been hired by the

Jockey Club to review all of the stables that had horses in the Century Race and make sure that we had abided by every one of their nitpicking rules. Now, sir, that was nothing but balderdash. Other than providing a smokescreen for your intentions, you have nothing whatsoever to do with the lords of Newmarket. My contacts in Scotland Yard have let me know that you are investigating the suspicious deaths of Nester Leggatt, and the two of Colonel Ross's men who died in the fire …"

"Oh, please, Mr. Holmes," he continued. "Do not be surprised. I am not in the least bit offended. You are a private consulting detective, and being deceitful is a necessary part of your *modus operandi*. And you have my respect and admiration. So, please, sir, let us dispense with the pretense and just get straight to the point, shall we? Begin your interrogation, please, sir. The floor is yours."

If Holmes was taken aback, he did not show it. He nodded slowly in agreement and with characteristic aplomb did as requested.

"Very well, sir," he responded. "Let us assume that I am accusing you of directly or indirectly murdering those three men. Please give me whatever evidence there is that would persuade me to conclude otherwise. The floor is yours, sir."

"Brilliant, and well done, Mr. Holmes," the baron replied. "No shilly-shallying around. But permit me a moment to begin on this excellent wine my steward has brought us. Ah, yes. A fine Margaux Bordeaux from 1875. Splendid. You will join me, sir? Wonderful. Now then, you want me to tell you why I would commit financial suicide. That is what you requested, is it not? Very well then, sir, it runs like this. It cost me nearly £5000 to secure the services of Nester Leggatt. He was the finest jockey in the country and was in demand by all of the owners. I offered him the top price, and he devoted six months to training and riding my horse, Lord Commodore. With his death, I had to move very quickly to find another jockey, which I did. The chap I found, Nat Archer, is perhaps a bit past his prime but an excellent man. He did his best, but a horse and rider take some time to get used to each other, and he had only a few days.

83

"I would like to believe that my horse, Lord Commodore, would have done much better with his familiar jockey. Now Colonel Ross's ghost horse ran a magnificent race, but I would wager that Lord Commodore could have given him a run for the money and allowed me to claim the Blue Riband. The loss hurt me in that place where I do hate to be injured, which is not the pocketbook, but my reputation. If you can provide any reason why I would have acted so foolishly, sir, do tell. I am all ears."

Holmes ignored the challenge and moved on. "The destruction of Mr. Silver and the murder of the two men. That would be in your financial interest, would it not?"

"Of course, it would. Lord Commodore is now the number one horse in the country for breeding fees. I will likely gain at least another £5000 a year because the white horse is out of the running. Not wishing to be pompous, sir, but in this business, such an amount is sweating. Rank sweating. Any man who is moved to risk the gallows for such a paltry amount has no business owning a first-class stable that aims to produce Cup winners. Forgive me, sir, if I say that my reaction to any such accusation is that I would be merely miffed that you assumed that Mapleton Stables was no more than just another set of barns delivering a herd of also-rans. I have become, I dare say with some pride, not only the leading stable in the nation for winning thoroughbreds, but also the only one with a reputation for being an enlightened employer of staff from throughout the Empire, regardless of age, race or gender. I would be a fool to risk that hard-earned reputation for a measly £5000 a year. Now sir, is there anything else you wish to know? No? Very well, then. I have given instructions to all of my employees that they must speak freely to you and give full and candid replies to whatever you wish to ask them."

At this point, he took another large swallow of his wine and turned to me. "My good doctor, I see you are enjoying your Bordeaux. Please, allow me to top up your glass." He snapped his fingers and one of his attentive staff, a handsome young lad in the same uniform as the rest of his colleagues, moved immediately to put more wine into my glass. As he was doing so, another one of the help, a beautiful young woman who I assumed had been recruited somewhere in the Orient, appeared bearing two plates of perfectly presented *canard confit*. These were laid in front of Holmes and me, but nothing appeared for our host.

Baron Julian then stood up and gave a shallow bow to us. "I really must ask you to excuse my terrible manners as a host, but I must now leave you to enjoy your lunch. I have some awfully pressing business related to some of our properties in the Cape. So kindly, as my guests, enjoy your lunch and dessert and a glass of excellent brandy. There is no rush for your departure. My man will take you to the train station whenever you wish to depart. And now let me excuse myself and wish you a splendid visit to the Cotswolds and Mapleton. Good day, gentlemen."

He smiled at us one more time, turned, and retreated into his manor house.

Holmes hastily finished his lunch and, declining the kind offerings of the help, thanked them and called for the driver. He said nothing to me during the drive back to the train station, and only once inside our cabin did he stop chewing harshly on his pipe and settle back into his seat.

"I do not," he said, "begrudge young Biggleswade his arrogant manipulation of charm and cavalier manners. Such skills are bred into our aristocrats from the moment they are born. What has deeply angered me is the egregious lack of secrecy at Scotland Yard. Gregson and Lestrade gave me this assignment, and they have been so absurdly careless as to let it become known. I will have to have a word with them on that."

"Rightly so," I added. "But what of his defense? I thought he did a rather good job of showing how absurd it would be for him to kill his own jockey or anybody else for that matter. Would you agree?"

Holmes took another slow draft on his pipe before answering. "Although I find his type of young nobleman to be repulsive, I must agree that I cannot possibly ascribe a reasonable motive to him.

However, someone, somewhere must have had a reason for these crimes, and it must have been a very powerful one to risk swinging by your neck if found out. As of this moment, I regret to say, I have no clear insight into what that might have been."

That was all he said until we returned to Paddington. He sat in silence with his chin upon his chest, and his brows knitted. The lovely late fall day had vanished, and storm clouds had moved in. By the time we arrived at the station, the rain was falling, and the wind was coming in gusts. The clock had not yet passed five, and Holmes insisted that I join him for tea and a chat by the fire in Baker Street. The dear Mrs. Hudson welcomed me warmly as she always did and hastened to put on the kettle and organize some light fare.

We were in the middle of the repast when a knock came to the door on Baker Street, and Mrs. Hudson appeared a few moments later bearing a telegram. She handed it to Holmes and made a comment about the poor lad who had to bring it through the storm. Holmes read it and scowled, his face clearly indicating his anger.

"This is an outrage," he said. "Lestrade's office is leaking like a sieve. Here, read this."

He tossed the telegram in my direction. It ran:

```
If you have returned from the Cotswolds
by the time this arrives, please join me
at Brooks's for a round of Port. I am
quite certain that I am next on your
list of suspects.

            Atherstone
```

"A bit of a surprise," I observed. "I assume that you are now on your way to St. James, storm or no. If I can be of assistance, I shall be happy to tag along."

"Of course, you must come. I would be lost without my Boswell."

"Are you sure," I asked, "that they will allow entry to the likes of us. We commoners are not quite up to snuff for that place."

Holmes smiled. "I expect that we shall be paraded as curiosities, much as if we were an exotic species from Africa. Come now. Let us be off."

Chapter Eight

Down the Hill

rooks's Club on St. James is one of the oldest and most exclusive of gentlemen's redoubts in London. Unlike White's, which was home to the bluest of blueblood Tories, whose positions in society and inherited wealth were a result only of their accident of birth, Brooks was the domain of progressive, enlightened liberals and Whigs, whose who positions in society and inherited wealth were also a result only of their accident of birth. Among its members were the two wealthiest men in England, Hugh Grosvenor, Duke of Westminster, and Lionel de Rothschild, the lord of just about everything that involved money. Sir Robert Peel, who had organized the police force, was an active member, as was Lord Earl Grey, who some years later was exiled to Canada. In a previous generation, Beau Brummell had been one of its most dashing members.

After taking a cab from Baker Street and through Mayfair, we arrived at the unmarked black door. We had neither umbrellas nor mackintoshes, and we waited in the cab, hoping that the rain would abate for a few minutes and allow us to dash inside. We admitted defeat and scrambled across the pavement, taking on a gallon of water before rushing through the door. We were greeted by a smiling doorman, who in turn, handed us off to a smiling porter.

"Ah, the one and only Mr. Sherlock Holmes, accompanied as always by Dr. Watson. We were rather pleased to get the note from Lord Atherstone, saying that you might be making a visit. Thank you, gentlemen, for gracing our establishment on such a miserable evening. The old boys are frightfully fond of your stories. Before I call for His Lordship, do allow me to introduce you to some of our members."

Before he could do so, one of the members who had been sitting near to the door, leaped to his feet and accosted us. He was holding in his outstretched hand a new copy of *The Adventure of Sherlock Holmes,* a collection of some of my past stories that my agent had recently arranged to have printed. I recognized the member as one of England's most popular novelists.

"Sherlock Holmes and Dr. Watson," he said enthusiastically. "Wonderful to have you here. Please, I must have you sign a copy of your book for me. It will have a treasured place on my bookshelf, I assure you."

He thrust the book at Holmes, who took it grudgingly. The fellow continued chatting to us.

"Oh, my, your coats are soaked. Has the weather turned bad?"

"The night has become dark and stormy," said Holmes as he reached for the pen on the porter's desk.

"Indeed," I added. "The rain is falling in torrents. Not letting up except when checked by violent gusts of wind that are sweeping up the streets. The tops of the houses are rattling, and the streetlights are being blown out. Perfectly beastly."

I took the book from Holmes, who had deigned only to inscribe *S. Holmes.* I scribbled *To Edward Bulwer-Lytton: a wonderful novelist,* signed my name and handed it back to the chap. He beamed a smile, thanked us profusely, and walked back to the sitting room. After a few steps, he stopped, put his finger to his chin, cocked his head, and then walked forward again slowly. We must have given him something to think about.

Without waiting any longer, the porter now took Holmes by the elbow and led him into the front sitting room where two score or more men were sitting around tables and chatting. The porter called for their attention and introduced us. We were greeted by a warm round of applause and loud and unpleasant oaths from some older chap in the corner. This led to a round of laughter and another round of applause.

The porter explained. "Lord Cavendish had made a bet that you would never arrive. He just lost 100 guineas to Lord St. Levan."

I had read that Brooks's Club had a reputation for the most esoteric bets. I recalled that a century ago, a certain Lord Cholmondeley had wagered Lord Derby that he could not, while in a balloon at least one thousand yards above the Earth, engage in a common human activity known to lead to procreation. The convivial atmosphere rather lifted my mood, and I could not resist smiling back at the porter.

Holmes was having none of it. He had not stopped scowling since reading the telegram.

"We are here to meet with Lord Atherstone," he said to the porter. "Kindly let him know of our arrival forthwith."

A few minutes later, the porter returned, followed by an elderly gentleman. The old fellow was well-dressed, nearly bald, somewhat stooped over and leaning on a walking stick. Upon reaching us, he turned to the porter.

"Right, Billy, say again who these two chaps are." The porter repeated our names.

"Right, yes, of course. Did I send a note off to you? Was that yesterday? Or today, perhaps? I cannot, for the life of me remember. Yes, yes, please come this way."

He turned and started unsteadily down a hallway, muttering back to us as he did.

"There is a room down this hall. Or at least, I think it is this hall. If not, then it must be the other one. We only have two. I reserved it for your visit. At least, I think I did, but perhaps I only intended to. Oh bother, if I didn't, we shall just have to meet somewhere. Oh yes, here it is. Do come in and sit down. Now then, which of you is Holmes?"

"I am Sherlock Holmes," said Holmes.

"Oh, good. You're the detective fellow, aren't you? What do you think of that dreadful business in Sumatra? Giant rats and all sorts of bizarre reports. Frankly, I think the zookeeper did it. What do you think, Mr. Holmes?"

Holmes said nothing but sat back and lit a cigarette. "Lord Atherstone, please drop the doddering old fool routine. I have neither the patience nor the time for it. You have one of the finest minds in the country and, I know from very reliable sources, it is as keen as ever."

The old fellow gave a look of feigned surprise, but then sat up and smiled broadly at Holmes.

"Ah, Mr. Holmes. You are such a spoilsport. You have no idea how thrilling it is at seventy-five years of age to have everyone assume that you either cannot hear what they are saying, or if you can then that your brains are so addled that you cannot understand. I recommend it to you when you reach my age. I must assume that your know-it-all older brother spilled the beans about me. He really is an insufferable prig. And yes, I confess that like Moses, my eye has not dimmed nor my natural force abated. And I do thank you for coming on such short notice."

"Enough of the pleasantries," said Holmes. "Why did you summon me? Please state your case, sir."

The old chap smiled back at Holmes. "My dear boy, you are far too young to be taking life so seriously. Here, have a glass of claret. It will cheer you up, and I will tell you my thoughts on this matter."

He stood and walked quickly, without his cane, over to the sideboard, and returned with wine glasses and a bottle. He began his story while pouring the drinks.

"There are only a hundred or so of us, Mr. Holmes. I refer to those of us who are fortunate to own stables of sufficient merit to breed and train horses that can rise through their conditions to the stakes level. We are all terribly competitive with each other, which we must be; otherwise, what would be the point of a horse race? But when threatened, we are rather like those muskoxen in the Arctic. You have seen pictures of them, no doubt. When attacked, they bring their backsides together and form a phalanx of horns against their attackers. When we heard that there was some talk about cheating and foul play, well, we were all very upset. None of us raise and race our horses for the money. Any that do are idiots. It is a ridiculously expensive hobby, and we all compete only for pride of place. For the glory. There is nothing quite like the thrill of standing in the winner's circle with your horse and jockey and being handed a plate or a cup and cheered on. If there is cheating involved, then it all falls apart. What pride can a man have if his horse wins by cheating? It ruins the whole sport. That is why the Jockey's Club was set up a century back, and we use it to make sure that everything is always on the up and up. Do you understand what I am saying, Mr. Holmes?"

"I do understand, but I fail to see the point that you are making."

The old fellow sat back and folded his arms across his chest. "The point, Mr. Holmes, is precisely that there is no point. Several of us have talked it over, and we simply cannot make any sense of it. What possible reason could there be for anyone to murder the best jockey in the land, on a strongly favored horse just before the race, and then to kill that magnificent white horse and its trainer and groom after the race? None of us can see any possible way that anyone would gain by doing so. It makes no sense, sir. That is the point."

"I see," said Holmes. "Then, if you have chatted about these matters with your friends, I am fairly certain that you have also identified any possible suspects, remote or otherwise. Will you kindly tell me what you have concluded?"

Lord Atherstone looked decidedly uncomfortable. "It is very poor form to say anything unproven about a man behind his back. Not an honorable way to act, Mr. Holmes. However, since you have asked, I will tell you that we suspected that no one in England could possibly have done the crime. And, having eliminated all other possibilities, as you have instructed us to do, the only remaining one must be the culprit. And the only ones left are the Americans. You must have noticed that they were all over the place, a few of the owners and an unholy gaggle of their agents. I cannot begin to speculate as to their motives, but it is possible that they may have had their reasons that are completely unknown to us. That was all we could come up with."

"That is useful, sir," said Holmes. "Now permit me another pointed question. I was disturbed to find that someone in Scotland Yard had informed you of the true nature of our investigation. If there is a traitor in the Yard, then he has to be exposed and stopped immediately. Otherwise, the integrity of justice is irreparably compromised. I need to know the source of your information."

On hearing this, his lordship looked bewildered. "Scotland Yard? Nonsense. It wasn't them at all. You paid a visit to Colonel Ross a few days back, and he immediately sent telegrams to the rest of us who had horses in the race telling us about your visit. We, in turn, passed the information along to the rest of our coterie. By now, every stable owner in England is aware of it. Terribly sorry to disappoint you, my dear boy, but there are no spies and no traitors hiding under the carpet."

Holmes took a slow sip from his glass of port, placed it on the table, and brought his hands together in front of his chest, his fingertips pressed against each other. "You are aware, I am sure, that I also paid a visit to Baron Julian, the son of Lord Biggleswade."

"Of course," replied his lordship. "And did he show off all his magnificent horses and stables and pretty young boys and girls? Ah, I see the answer on your face. And treat you to an exquisite lunch and a bottle of rare old wine? Oh, yes, I see he did. He does the gracious host thing rather well, does he not? He does it to all of us, especially to those we know he positively cannot stand. Welcome to the club, Mr. Holmes. So, yes, what about your visit to Julian?"

"The man explicitly told me that the information concerning my visit was provided to him by his contacts inside Scotland Yard. You have now informed me that it came from an entirely different source. Now, sir, I must know which of you is telling me the truth – and I suspect it is you – and why young Biggleswade would lie to me?"

With this, Lord Atherstone burst out laughing. "Oh really, Holmes. You mustn't take Julian so seriously. He has done a brilliant job with his stables and horses, but he is a silly boy who imagines himself a dashing spy, a womanizer, a Lord Byron, Nathan Hale, and Casanova all rolled into one. We tolerate his vain imaginings. His father was much the same in his day. It will only be a matter of a few more years before age and gravity take their toll, and he becomes portly and balding like the rest of us. He is a brilliant breeder and a pathetic braggadocio. A silly short, rich boy who wants to be a hero. Please, Holmes, take no count of him."

He laughed again and gulped back the rest of his port. We thanked him for his time and hospitality and departed into the still beastly weather that was besetting London.

Over a period of twenty years, I have reported on many cases presented to and solved by Sherlock Holmes. Some were of monumental importance to the state, others were significant only because they demonstrated the ingenuity of evil men in plotting their crimes and the brilliance and tenacity of Sherlock Holmes in solving their crimes and bringing justice down upon the heads.

It would be appropriate if at this juncture in my account of the murders associated with the Century Race I were to show you how Sherlock Holmes synthesized so many diverse strands of evidence, deduced from the data the connections which his creative mind and tireless imagination saw in them – so unapparent to the rest of us – and how he triumphed, identified the villains and dragged them into court, possibly with some minor assistance from Scotland Yard.

I would like to be able to write about that, but I cannot.

Sherlock Holmes failed.

After our interview with Lord Atherstone, Holmes diligently spoke with many other racehorse owners, track officials, tic-tac men, bookies, punters, and anyone else associated with horseracing that he thought might have some insight into the horrible events of the autumn of 1899.

It was all for naught. By Christmas, he was no nearer to a solution than he had been the day after the race. There were many characters who were part of the racing populace. More than a few of them might have been willing to bend a few of the rules in order to improve their odds of winning, but none had sufficient motive to do murder.

Holmes readily agreed that the American contingent would be more than somewhat happy to put a fix into a race, but the killing of such a magnificent animal as Mr. Silver was anathema to them. A bookie or two might get "bumped off" but doing serious harm to horses was definitely off-limits.

Toward the end of the Michaelmas term, a letter came from Scotland Yard officially dismissing Holmes from the case and suggesting that he should not consider submitting his usual fee since he had not brought forward a scrap of new evidence.

Early in the new year, when England and all of the world was celebrating the beginning of the twentieth century, a note arrived from Robert Blinden. He was crushed by the ignominy heaped upon him for his role in the terrible fire at Epsom and had decamped for

America. He had found work in a very fine stables in the State of Kentucky, where, he informed us, everyone was quite mad about racehorses. He was, he assured us, for the first time in his life, being treated with respect regardless of his appearance, but he thought it was a result less of the enlightenment of the owners than the presence of a surprising number of chaps who looked much like he did.

A year passed and still nothing. Holmes was hired for several other cases in which he performed brilliantly, and I was honored to have assisted him to a trifling degree and to enjoy the celebration that each success brought. The celebrations did not last long, and all too often, I saw Holmes sitting and again reviewing the files concerning the Derby fire and murders. On many occasions, I caught him reading the *Sporting News,* and I was certain that he was being eaten up inside by his memory of that case.

Once, in early 1901, I tried to make light of the case, now two years in the past. Holmes snapped at me for doing so.

"Watson," he barked, "three men were murdered. They all had wives and families and years of life to look forward to. I fail to see how you can make it a matter of jest."

That was the last time I tried that tact.

Later that year, our dear Queen Victoria passed away after serving for longer than any monarch in the history of England. We all knew she could not go on living forever, and there was a universal sentiment that time was passing, and things in the world were, with a few exceptions, going the way they should. A new king, Edward VII, ascended the throne in the summer of 1902, and a wonderfully optimistic era was upon us.

Holmes had traveled extensively in the early years of the twentieth century. One voyage took him first to Odessa at the request of Czar Nicholas, and then to Ceylon to sort out the tragedy of the Atkinson brothers, and as far as Sumatra, to deal with a rodent of unusual size. He made several trips over to the Continent and received numerous honors for his exceptional service to the heads of at least three states.

And yet ... as soon as a case was over and put into the filing case, he once again returned to this elusive puzzle, and its ghost horse, and murders devoid of any conceivable motive.

Chapter Nine

Neck and Neck

A full five years had passed when on a miserable November evening, I chanced to find myself sitting by a crackling fire and enjoying a brandy with Holmes. Our idle chit-chat about some of the cases I had written up led me to ask about the events that had taken place in Epsom.

"Any leads at all on that one, Holmes?" I queried.

"Nothing. It keeps coming back to haunt me, but I am still where I was in my deductions five years back."

"And where was that?"

"The only person with any motive at all was the colonel, for the insurance. He certainly did not seem the type to commit such a monstrous crime, but I have learned that the type men seem and the deeds they do are often far removed from each other, and when that fellow was on the battlefield he did not flinch at sending men into firefights where they were certain to die. So I cannot entirely rule him out."

I do not, as a rule, contradict Sherlock Holmes as I have learned time and time again that his logic is invariably brilliant, but, this time, I felt there was something I simply had to say to him.

"Holmes, there is something you should know about Ross."

"Indeed, and pray tell what is that?"

"You are aware that in my medical practice, I have quite a few veterans of the BEF."

"Yes Watson, I am aware of that. It is common among veterans to seek a doctor who shared their experience. Not at all surprising that they found you."

"You are aware as well that we veterans are honor-bound that we do not tell tales out of school, but that among ourselves, there are no secrets, and we are rather terrible gossips."

"Yes Watson, and I presume that this is leading somewhere. Kindly get to the point."

"Many of the chaps I see served under Ross in India and Afghanistan. I did not, as he was not connected to the Northumberland Fusiliers. He took over command of the 51st, the Yorkshire Lights, when General Browne was wounded. Within six months, he had whipped them into an elite brigade that was fearless, moved at lightning speed, and absolutely brilliant in their strategies."

"And was he loved and admired by his men?"

"No. Not at all. But feared and respected. He was one of the hardest men in the entire BEF. As flexible as an iron ramrod. His discipline was demanding and brooked not even the most minuscule infraction. In the first few months, men in his unit were flogged regularly. One was even put before a firing squad for cowardice. But they became the toughest and most disciplined unit in the campaign. His men did not like him in the least, but they admired and feared him no end. Within a year, they had become one of the proudest group of soldiers I had ever met."

"So, are you confirming my statement," said Holmes, "that he did hesitate to send men into battle, knowing that some would not return? Or even have his own men shot. What, pray tell, is it you are trying to say?"

"Many of his men were so badly wounded that they will spend the rest of their days in hospital. Ross spends every Sunday visiting them in Royal Chelsea, or St. Tom's or wherever they may be confined."

"That is lovely, Watson. Are you saying that he missed his calling and should have been a parson instead of an officer in the BEF?"

"No, those chaps are all looked after by their veterans' pensions, but there are twenty or so soldiers who will never find work because their minds are gone. Shell shock, you know. But they receive no pension because the fools in Whitehall have concluded that all those chaps have to do is snap out of it and stop malingering."

"That is very sad indeed, Watson. Although not surprising."

"What is surprising is that Colonel Ross supports every one of those fellows out of his own pocket. Every month their families receive a stipend directly from him. He does not let on, being one of those men who believes that the left hand should not know what the right is doing. You know the type."

"Yes, all the more likely to result in his needing money from the insurance on his horse."

"Oh yes, I was getting to that. All that money from Lloyds, do you know what he did with it?"

"No Watson, although it appears you are about to tell me if you ever get to that point in your story."

"He put it all into two trusts. One for the family of the trainer and one for the family of the groom. The income from those trusts goes to them. He has not drawn a farthing from it. I thought you might like to know about that."

Holmes gave me a less than friendly look for several seconds. "Thank you, Watson. You have successfully removed my only suspect from my list, and now I am left with none. Yes, thank you indeed."

From time to time, Holmes could be sarcastic.

Several months later, on a pleasant day in the spring of 1905, I caught up again with Holmes for lunch in St. John's Wood, and he invited me back to 221B Baker Street for an afternoon round of brandy. While climbing the familiar seventeen stairs up to the room in which he and I had passed so many fine evenings before I moved out to live with my lovely wife, we were met a few steps from the top by the redoubtable Mrs. Hudson. She raised her hand, bidding us pause our ascent.

"You have some visitors, Mr. Holmes. Passing strange ones, they are. Americans. They've been waiting for an hour and say that they must see you. I brought them cups of tea, and didn't they go and pull flasks from their pockets and fill the cup to the brim with whiskey. At least, the two men did. There's a young woman with them too, who seems a bit more refined. But they are an odd lot, I must say."

I followed Holmes into the room and was, I must admit, somewhat pleasantly surprised by who I saw standing to greet us. Two of the three Americans we had met in Epsom five years ago were waiting. Along with them was an exceptionally attractive, tall, young woman. She was dressed in a very American style with a tight gray skirt that only reached a little past her knees, a matching gray suit jacket, a brilliant starched white shirt, the arms of which extended past the cuffs of her jacket and bore a brilliant set of silver cufflinks. Around her neck, she had a delicate gold chain to which a gold cross was attached, and which bobbed back and forth just beyond the tops of a bosom that would fill a Greek goddess with envy.

The fellow who had worn the yellow suit during our earlier encounter, and whose name I could not recall, was now dressed in a far more somber dark blue suit, a modest white shirt, and a striped blue long necktie. The third member, who I could only remember by the nickname of "Sorrowful" was also dressed in business-like attire, with a black suit, white shirt, and black tie. The chap, formerly the bearer of the yellow suit, crossed the floor and greeted us.

"Hey, a big hello to Mr. Sherlock Holmes and hello to you too, Doc. It is an honor for us to be back here in this here London and to reacquaint ourselves with you. You, I am sure, remember my esteemed colleague, Mr. Archibald Jones, although he is much better known by the appellation of Sorrowful. And he is the honorary father to this gorgeous young doll, who is his honorary daughter, which is a more than somewhat fascinating story all in itself which perhaps we can tell you over a round of ale at your local watering place. Allow me briefly to say that she is known to us as Little Miss Marker except that she is no longer little, so we have reverted to calling her Markie, which you may wish to as well. If my memory serves me correctly, I believe that this time the drinks are on us."

The young lady laughed pleasantly and walked toward us, giving a smart smack to the backside of the chap in the blue suit.

"Oh you. You are incorrigible." Then she stepped up to Sherlock Holmes and extended her hand.

"Good afternoon, Mr. Holmes. I am Martha O'Connor. And Dr. Watson, a pleasure to meet you. I know you as if you were my next-door neighbors after reading all those stories. And please excuse my companions, they are really diamonds in the rough, and I love them dearly. And if you are wondering what a nice girl like me is doing in their company, I promise to explain it to you over a beer at your local pub. Shall we go, gentlemen?"

Holmes looked perplexed for a minute but then smiled and nodded. We turned and descended the stairs and sauntered along Baker Street in the direction of Marylebone. The chap in the blue suit chatted on about the weather in London, recalling that his last night here five years ago was one of the darkest and stormiest he could remember, and how he was thankful that at the moment it was not raining. Holmes was, I knew, not listening but most likely was overwhelmed with memories and thoughts about the case of the murders at Epsom. Sorrowful said nothing, and I had the pleasure of walking beside Miss Markie, or Martha, or whatever she wished to be called. She had put her hat on her head, a wide-brimmed one with a small net that partially covered her face, and she looked positively splendid. It occurred to me that had I been so fortunate as to have been the father to a daughter, I would have been thrilled to have one so attractive and pleasant as the one who was walking by my side.

"I am afraid," I said to her, "that once we reach the pub, the conversation will be dominated by your friend. So please, you must tell me how in heaven's name you ended up with these fellows."

She let loose with a peal of pleasant laughter and then smiled warmly at me, slipped her arm through mine, and began her story.

"Well Doctor, it all began when I was five years old. One fateful afternoon my parents departed for an extended stay in Japan where daddy was to be the new ambassador, and I was left in the care of my nanny and an aging guardian. That afternoon my chauffeur was driving me to my aunt's, and he stopped beside a bar on Broadway and ran inside. It must have been to borrow some money that he then placed as a bet on a horse, and as he had nothing else to leave as his marker, he left me, promising to return within the hour with the money to pay back the loan and retrieve me."

"That," I noted, "is a highly unusual way to secure a debt, even in America, is it not."

She laughed again. "What is more unusual is that he never came back. To this day, I have no idea what happened to him. I can only guess that the long arm of the law was on his tail, and he scampered off to St. Louis or goodness knows where. But he left me in the care of this wonderful gentleman who is walking in front of us, Mr. Archibald Jones, or Sorrowful to all who know him, and he had no idea what to do with me, so he just took care of me. We had a wonderful apartment on West 49th, just off Seventh Avenue. Sorrowful became like a father, and I was mothered by all sorts of dear women who sang and danced and served tables in the nightclubs, and some who did none of those things but who had other talents for which they were well paid. Everyday Sorrowful would take me to the racetrack or the zoo or the Museum of Natural History or the Met Museum. Somedays we would picnic in Central Park. I cannot remember a single day of being unhappy. It was a dream world. At night, I would go with them to the local nightclub, and they would put me up on stage and tell me to sing. So I did, and they all cheered. It was a world away from the Upper East Side and I reveled in every minute of it."

"Good heavens," I blurted out, "Where were your parents? Your guardians? Why … you were abandoned."

"Oh my, yes, I was and could not have been happier. My nanny thought my parents must have decided at the last minute to take me to Japan, and they thought I was with my nanny and aunt, and frankly, they were all too busy with their diplomatic life to even think about me. It went on like that for three whole years and might have gone longer had I not gotten terribly sick. I almost died."

"My word, what happened?"

"Oh, I cannot remember much, but I had a terrible fever and pneumonia and goodness know what else and Sorrowful, and Harry had to go into the Upper East Side and kidnap the best pediatrician in New York at gunpoint and make him come and look after me, which he did, of course as anyone would with two guns stuck into your ribs. He immediately shipped me off to the Bellevue, and then all hell broke loose, as they say. The police and the courts and the doctors and the government all got excited about this poor abandoned little girl. They summoned my parents back from Japan. It was all they could do to keep it out of the press. My mom had fifty fits. Would have made such a great scandal. Don't you think, doctor?"

"I must say, I imagine it would have."

"So then I was back home and forced to attend P.S. 267 every day. But by then, I knew my way all over Manhattan, so I would walk in the front door of the school and out the back and be down at Mindy's at Broadway and West 49th a half-hour later. And the next day, I would waltz into the school and hand them the most exquisitely forged note or certificate from a doctor, or a dentist, or a piano teacher explaining my absence.

"My parents sent me to Hunter College, which was absolutely a divine choice. There is a subway station right underneath it. I would jump onto the 4/5/6 line, and in no time, I could be on the F train and out to the Aqueduct or Belmont in an hour."

Here Sorrowful, who had been listening to the story, turned around and spoke.

"And she turns out to be the best handicapper in all of New York City."

I was obviously looking puzzled by that news, and Miss Martha explained.

"Betting on the races is nothing but arithmetic. Sorrowful and Harry taught me how to do it, and by the time I was in my junior year, I was a whiz. I would read the daily form, look at the morning line and tell the fellows who to bet on and how much. And most of the time, we won, didn't we, Sorrowful?"

"We are winners almost every time, kid. We are making so much scratch that we are now become respectable and dignified members of New York society, and our Little Miss Marker is so smart that she is off to college. Isn't that right, kid?"

"I have a scholarship to Radcliffe to study mathematics. But I demanded that I have my grand tour of Europe first. Well, mom had fifty fits, and I had to throw a temper tantrum for two days before she agreed. So off I went to Europe with my guardian, who is terrible with her directions and somehow keeps getting lost for several days at a time. Where did we leave her last, Sorrowful?"

"In the big place with all those paintings across from the guy on the tower with the lions."

"And so," Miss Martha said, "here I am, with my dear honorary father and his fine friend, and we are on a mission to find some mysterious horse."

By this time, we were south of Marylebone, and Holmes had led us a block west to one of his preferred local establishments, the

105

Beehive Pub, a congenial place with good ale, plenteous food, and a crackling fireplace.

We sat and ordered a round of drinks. I looked at Miss Martha in unabashed admiration. She had an angelic face and was no more than eighteen years of age, but I had a sense that there was not much that this young woman had not already seen or was prepared to deal with if necessary, as long as her mother never heard about it.

The chap in the blue suit acted, as he had five years ago, as the chairman of our little assembly.

"It is a pleasure to re-acquaint ourselves with our illustrious and famous friends, Mr. Watson and Doctor Holmes."

Before he could continue, Holmes interrupted him.

"Where's Harry?"

"I am glad you made that thoughtful inquiry, sir. Our dear friend, Harry-the-Horse, is now a very hot item in all of New England. The local constabulary for reasons that we cannot comprehend are saying that a certain Brinks truck ended up swimming in the East River, and they are thinking that Harry has something to do with this strange occurrence. I say we cannot comprehend their logic as we all know that Harry does not know how to swim, not even enough to get from a yacht to the shore with a bag of jewels attached to him. But because he is very hot, he has found it necessary to vacate our fine city and spend some quiet time reflecting on the beauty of nature somewhere north of Maine. I am sure he would send his regards if he knew that we are visiting his friends in London. So, greetings from Harry *in absentia*."

He raised his glass, and we toasted Harry. The chap then continued his introduction to our meeting.

"When I am departing from England after our previous visit I am thinking that never again am I coming back here nor do I think that I would ever again want to, as our last visit is not particularly a pleasant one, what with guys getting roasted and a fine racehorse getting all braised and toasted. But here we are, and we are once again acting on behalf of a syndicate whose in needs we have a pecuniary interest.

"As you know, sirs, we are devoted participants in the sport of kings. Thus, it is imperative and also very important that we are cognizant of all the details about many horses else we could not be good handicappers, only lousy touts, and we would go bust. So we are every day looking at the racing newspapers from all across the great United States of America and watching to see what horses are winning and what horses are losing and what the conditions are when they win and who was their sire and this and that and so on and so forth. Almost all the names of all the horses and all the stables and all the trainers are familiar to us. However, starting three years ago, we see that a maiden three-year-old wins a race out in L A, and beside his name is the name of his sire, and it says, *Sir Galahad*. Now I do not know any sire in America by that name, and it is quite understandable because beside the name of the sire in brackets, it says E N G followed by a period and another bracket. This means that the sire is in England, and that is sufficient and necessary cause for why I do not know his name. This is not a problem because all the time stallions and dams are being moved all over the world to breed with each other on account of because incest is not a good thing for horses any more than it is for humans. So, I am not concerned that I do not know this sire.

"Then two weeks later again I see that a horse in St. Louis wins his maiden race and his sire is again Sir Galahad in England. So, I can see that this English horse has some good things going for him and I make a note to be looking out for him again in the future. Well, the future comes very quickly, because a week later there he is again as daddy to a winner in Hialeah. And next, he shows up at the Hawthorne in Chicago. And then he is way up there in Montreal where it is almost too cold for humans or horses, but he is sire to a winner who even has a French name.

"By the end of the season, I am seeing eighteen maiden horses who are sired by Sir Galahad and are winners, and I am thinking that this must be one excellent sire. So, I begin to lay a few bets on his progeny, and they pay off handsomely. The next year I am watching again for Sir Galahad's name, and there he is again, not only for the four-year-olds, but now for a whole new crop of three-year-olds, and again I lay my bets on these horses, and I am making very serious scratch. By the end of the year, I am now counting over forty horses across America from sea to sea who have Sir Galahad as their daddy.

"Now I know that some serious research is being called for, so I get in touch with my esteemed colleague, Sorrowful, and I ask him if I can borrow his kid for a week, by his kid I am referring to his honorary daughter who has now become a very lovely young doll and who is also very very smart, and is now gracing us with her presence at this table. I ask Little Miss Marker, who is no longer little but tall and gorgeous, if she can check out all of Sir Galahad's offspring across America, which she does. She reads all the forms from all the racetracks, and she reports back to me that there are sixty racehorses scattered across racetracks that list Sir Galahad of England as their sire. But then says that there is something very curious about these horses. They are running at over thirty tracks, but they all belong only to six owners, which is very odd indeed. I try to make contact with two of these guys, and I get a very cold shoulder from them. One even has me escorted out of his premises by a big galoot who is holding a Roscoe to the back of my head. The inside dope on Sir Galahad it seems is tighter than the nun's pajamas if you know what I mean.

"So I venture again to my old buddies Patience and Fortitude who are still there guarding the corner of Fifth and Forty-First, and I proceed up to Rosie's Room and again find the pleasant lady who is a doll even if she is no longer a very young doll and whose uncle was an excellent handicapper. I tell her that I need to look through all copies of *Sporting News* from England for the past few years to find out about this horse, Sir Galahad. She says to me that she can do this for me on company time paid for by the City of New York because that is her job as a librarian, and all I have to do is take her out for dinner. So this I do and, since I am now, thanks to my excellent year of beneficial betting, a gentleman of sorts, I not only take her out, but

I take her to Delmonico's and not to Mindy's. We have a very nice time and some of this and that afterward, and I call on her a few days later. She knocks me over when she says that no such horse as my Sir Galahad exists. She has looked through all the English papers for the past ten years, and there is not a single mention of such a horse.

"Well now, gentlemen, I am facing a serious problem which, if it is not resolved in my favor, could lead to unhappy consequences for my well-being. This is on account of because I speak to a big-shot owner who has many horses at Belmont, and I say to him that I have some inside dope on a sire whose progeny are winning many races. He listens to me not only because I am now well-dressed and have been seen in places like Delmonico's where I am previously not welcome, but also because he is a true sportsman who loves getting inside dope. I tell him it is all hush-hush, which he likes even more, and I lay out all my cards concerning Sir Galahad and the record of the winners that he has sired. I tell him that I am an expert on sires over in England since I am over there quite recently and, more than somewhat prematurely I must admit, I tell him that for a serious amount of potatoes I can arrange for one or two of his fine mares to be transported across The Pond and serviced by Sir Galahad. He is very happy with this opportunity and gives me a serious down-payment and tells me to get busy.

"So, without going into too many details, I tell the librarian doll that I am now dealing with a mystery since for sixty horses who are mostly winners to have a sire that does not exist is indeed highly mysterious. And she says to me, if I have a mystery to be solved in England, the man I must get to help me is the famous detective Sherlock Holmes. And I remember that I know that name because when I am in England, I get to know this Sherlock Holmes but even if he is a hotshot detective I remember that when it comes to horse racing, he is a complete chump who could not tell a horse's head from a horse's ass with two hands and a roadmap. But the librarian doll says that I am not needing a handicapper, I am needing a detective.

"Then I meet again with Little Miss Marker here, and she again says to me that I am looking at a very puzzling mystery over in England and she says that the man I must ask for help is Mr. Sherlock Holmes because after she recovered from reading about the tragic and sad death of Black Beauty, she then reads all these stories about Sherlock Holmes and how he solves mysteries especially those that are more than somewhat highly mysterious.

"But then something else even more peculiar happens. Miss Marker comes to me and tells me something that is stranger than strange and bordering on weird, which she will now relate to you on account of because I have been talking far too long and have not been able to enjoy my beer, which I shall now do."

He took a long draft of his ale and nodded toward Miss Martha. She flashed her radiant smile, laughed, and took up the story.

"Ah come on, it is not weird at all. There must be an explanation for it that we just do not yet know. It began when I came to my dear friend here and asked him how many racehorses in America were pure white in color. He told me that such a coloring is rare but not unknown, and that is because it is caused by a recessive gene, and it has about the same as the percentage as redheads among dolls, which is about two percent. At a busy racetrack, you might see one every two or three days, but not likely more often. And then I told him that for all of these offspring of Sir Galahad that I had found across the country, there was a ratio of one completely white horse for every five. When I told him that, he told me about the incredible horse, Mr. Silver, who had run so beautifully in the Century Race here a few years back, and how the poor thing died in the fire the same night as his victory, and that it was possible that Mr. Silver had a brother who might be none other than our mysterious Sir Galahad."

She smiled again, and the chap in the blue suit, having drained his glass of ale and called for another, took over.

"So, Mr. Sherlock Holmes, we are come to hire your detective services. We want you to find Sir Galahad."

Chapter Ten

Into the Home Stretch

I have come to know those subtle signs that Sherlock Holmes gives that say that he is as pleased as punch with whatever prospect has just been laid before him. This was one of those times. His hands came together in front of his chest, and with some difficulty, he struggled not to rub them together. His face affected a practiced smile of nonchalance. He was, to me, obviously delighted with the offer and straining not to be jumping up and down with glee.

"I suppose I could make myself available to assist you," he said. "I believe that I should be able to settle your affairs within a week or two. I will most likely have to call upon you for your participation and I will expect your enthusiastic support. If you are in agreement, then I suggest that we get started forthwith."

The three Americans spent a minute looking at each other, pursing their lips and nodding. The chap in the blue suit answered on their behalf.

"Okay, Sherlock. We have a deal. So what happens next?"

"The three of you remain here at the Beehive and enjoy your supper. They have an excellent pork loin. I highly recommend it. Dr. Watson and I shall leave you and begin our work. So, allow me to bid you good-day. I believe that you may be contacted care of the Metropole Hotel."

"Yeah, that is where we are," said Sorrowful.

Holmes and I left them sitting there, and I followed him as he walked quickly back towards 221B Baker Street. There was a gleam in his eyes and a suppressed excitement in his manner which convinced me, used as I was to his ways, that his hand was upon a clue, though I could not imagine where he had found it.

"Good heavens, Holmes," I sputtered as he led me on a forced march. "You know next to nothing about horse racing. How in the world are you going to find a horse that there is no record of within a week?"

"There is a record of it."

"So were these folks blind? They said that they had read every copy of the *Sporting News* for the past decade, and there was not a single mention of any Sir Galahad."

"They were looking in the wrong place."

He was being cryptic as he was often wont to be, and it was a waste of my time to ask any further. Once we reached Baker Street, he rushed immediately to one of the closets in which he stored his tin file boxes. He brought out three of them, labels bearing the *Sporting News* during the previous three years.

"My dear doctor," he muttered to me, and he rifled through the first box. "It may come as a surprise to you that I have not rested a day in my interest in the Epsom Downs tragedy. I have read every line of every issue of this miserable rag since that time. Contrary to your conclusions, I am now quite the expert on horse racing in England, and while my knowledge five years ago was feeble and close to non-existent, I must say that now it approaches encyclopedic. Our friends were quite correct in noting that there was no mention of Sir Galahad in the daily forms or the race results, but I recall two appearances of the name in what amounts to an agony column in this paper. It will take me a few minutes to locate it, but I know it is in here."

One issue after another, he opened them, scanned the back page, and put it down.

"Aha!" he cried. "Here it is. The 15 March issue of two years back. Have a look." He stabbed at the paper with his long thin forefinger and handed it to me.

A small note in the agony column read:

```
Dear  Sir  Galahad:  American  investor  in
need  of  your  services.  Will  pay  top
dollar.
```

Then he gave me the issue for the following week, in which came the reply.

```
Dear   American   Investor:   Contact   Sir
Galahad at Box 693, E.C.
```

"There they are," exulted Holmes. "We shall simply follow the example provided and see if they will respond to the bait."

He sat down into his armchair, drew his feet up under his body, brought his hands together in front of him, and closed his eyes. It was his customary pose when deep into concentration. I was quietly pleased to see traces of a smile from time to time at the corners of his mouth. After some fifteen minutes, he spoke to me.

"My dear friend, might you possibly be able, a week or so from today, to undergo an extensive disguise, and then to pretend that you are an Englishman who has moved to America and are now employed as the accountant to a horseracing syndicate?"

I assured him that I could do that and was rather delighted with the prospect.

"I shall have to be in disguise as well," he continued. "I believe I could be a convincing English bloke who has moved to America and is now a professional handicapper. Yes, I do believe I could do that. It will not be necessary to disguise our American clients, as they will only have to act the way all Americans do. Mind you, I don't know what to do about Lestrade. His theatrical skills are dreadful, but I shall think of something. And, of course, we shall need a horse."

Having said these things, he closed his eyes again. I did not have the faintest idea as to what he was stitching together in his most unusual brain, but my blood was already warming to the adventure. I must admit that even after twenty-five years, there was nothing that I enjoyed more in all of life than rushing into the game with Sherlock Holmes once it was afoot. And most certainly, it was now up and running.

He opened his eyes, rose, and scurried over to his writing desk and began to scribble something.

"My dear Watson, Could I kindly prevail upon you to drop this off at the post office on your way home? If you have it in by the end of the day today, we should be in time for the *Sporting News* issue on Sunday.

I agreed, and he handed me a brief note for insertion into the agony column. It ran:

```
Attention  Sir  Galahad:  Major  American
syndicate  requests  first  class  exclusive
services.  Immediate  response  requested.
Reply to Amer. Synd. Metropole Hotel.
```

"We will see if this does the trick," he said. "I shall let you know what transpires."

As I prepared to leave with this note in hand, I turned back to Holmes. "I am quite certain, Holmes, that you have no interest whatsoever in merely tracking down a mysterious horse. You must see some connection between this and the murders six years ago at Epsom."

"Is that not obvious, Watson?"

Chapter Eleven

The Finish Line

I had taken quite a shine to the spirited young Martha O'Connor, and, as there were a couple of days before our note in the *Sporting News* would be published, I made a point of inviting her to a lunch with me and my wife, Mary. She agreed and came the next day to our pleasant flat just off Marylebone. The three of us had a delightful conversation, hearing more of her unusual upbringing and her adventures in racetracks, nightclubs, gambling dens, and private schools. She had us in stitches for well over an hour. My wife, hoping I am sure to arrange another such encounter, asked if there were any place in London that she might like to visit.

"You might quite enjoy," said Mary, "the Victoria and Albert Museum, or the British Museum. You know it has all those lovely Elgin Marbles, and the Rosetta Stone, and that exquisite Portland Vase. Or might you like to watch the Changing of the Guard at Buckingham Palace?"

Miss Martha smiled back and for a second, quite uncharacteristically, blushed before speaking. "Oh, you will think that I am a terribly wayward and wanton young woman if I tell you what I am just dying to do."

"Well then, do tell," said Mary. "You have commanded my attention."

"It is just that all those lovely things you suggest are already on my itinerary and my governess will be making sure that I see every one of them. But there is one place I have heard of that sounds so unusual that I really must find out for myself."

"And what might that be?" I asked.

"Do you know of a place called Brooks's Club on a street named St. James?"

I was entirely taken aback. "Why, of course, I know it. I have visited several times over the years. But why, in heaven's name, would you want to visit a stuffy men's club?"

"Because I have heard that it is the pinnacle of all places on earth for outrageous gambling, where men are willing to stake fortunes on a hand of cards. It is quite famous for that, is it not?"

"Are you saying," I asked, somewhat disbelieving, "that you want to go and watch some of the wealthiest men in the world as they toss thousands of pounds back and forth across a gaming table? Is that what you wish to do?"

She dropped her head and blushed again. "No Doctor. Oh dear, this is terribly embarrassing. No, I do not want to watch them. I want to play them … and *beat* them."

My dear wife gasped in glee and clapped her hands together. "Oh, you are a girl after my own heart. Do you truly believe you could do that? Are you that good?"

"Sorrowful and all the guys who raised me taught me to play when I was five years old. I have never stopped. And, I do not wish to be boastful, but I am very, very good at it. I have trounced all of the high-stakes men in New York. Of course, the really rich men are too smart to keep losing, but there are many who were not as smart and now are more than somewhat poorer. I cannot get any of them to take me on anymore. This would be my dream, and I am so excited at the prospect. Is there any possible way, Dr. Watson, that you could get me in there?"

"My dear, I am so sorry, women are not permitted on the premises."

"Oh yes, I know that. But I read that there is an annex behind the club where they hold events for both men and women. Could we not set up a game there? I do believe, sir, that if a notice were posted that an American Girl challenged any man in the club to a round of poker, with an entry fee of £500 that it would create a bit of a buzz, would it not?"

"Five hundred pounds," I sputtered. "My dear girl, that is a fortune. Of course, it would arouse a tidal wave of interest. But my dear, can you really afford to spend that much? And what if you lose? You would be destitute, and they would come after your family demanding payment."

Again, she smiled, this time bordering on impish. "Well, yes, doctor, I can afford it. For the past five years, I have won consistently at cards and at the racetrack, and I am far from destitute."

"But what if you lose? It would be utterly distressing to you." I said.

"Then, I lose." She shrugged her shoulders and added, "And Doctor … real gamblers don't cry."

My wife immediately sided with Miss Martha, and with both of the arraigned against me, I had to give in. The three of us took a stroll toward Mayfair, and Mary and Miss Martha waited for me around the corner in the tea room of the St. James Hotel. Against my better judgment, I entered Brooks and asked for the two chaps I knew would be there. I was soon seated with an aging Lord Atherstone and my fellow writer, Edward Bulwer-Lytton. Before I could launch into my proposal, Ed opened his valise and brought out two copies of his latest novel, *Paul Clifford,* signed the title pages and handed them to me with a beaming smile.

"One for you and one for Holmes. You were my inspiration."

I had no idea what he was talking about and went ahead and placed my proposal in front of them.

Their reaction was like two schoolboys who had just been told that geometry class would be canceled so that they could watch a special cricket match. They slapped their thighs and pounded the table.

"Oh, splendid," wheezed the octogenarian Atherstone. "A capital idea. We have not had a good evening as that since Bertie stopped coming around."

"Let's go and place it before the General Secretary," proposed Bulwer-Lytton. "He can be a bit of a prude when it comes to activities that involve the weaker sex. He may be a bit of a sticky wicket."

The General Secretary of Brooks listened politely as we made our suggestion, but I detected a faint smile appearing on his otherwise featureless face.

"It may surprise you, sirs," he said stiffly, "if I told you that I have heard about this American girl. We general secretaries of the more exclusive clubs around the world all keep in touch with each other over matters of mutual concern. I have heard about this young lady from my colleagues in New York and Boston. She could provide us with a very memorable evening. I will approve this event, subject to some minor conditions."

"Very well," said Lord Atherstone, "spit them out, Georgie."

"One, that we must be fair and not limit the event to poker, which is a terribly American game. But she must agree that we shall alternate one round of poker, with one of whist, an English game. That would keep things fair. Two, that you agree that the invitation may be extended to members of White's, Reform, and Boodle's. Maybe The Athenaeum, and The Carlton too. And three, that the entry fee must be raised to £1,000, paid to the club. If we are going to have an event that will be talked about for years, then we had best go all out, should we not? Tomorrow night, shall it be? Start at six and carry on until sunrise, or until the lady drops out. What do you say?"

The other two agreed immediately. I felt trapped. This was altogether too rich for my blood, and I was overcome with worry as to what an enormous pit had been opened for this young and, I feared, over-confident woman from America.

I found the two of them chatting merrily over tea in the hotel and sat down. Gloom and doom must have been written all over my face.

"Oh darling," began my wife, "did they turn you down? Oh, I am so sorry."

I shook my head and whispered, "No. Worse. They accepted." I fearfully recited the conditions, shaking my head in despair as I did so. When I finished, I looked up at Miss Martha, who was positively beaming with joy.

"Oh, Doctor Watson. How can I thank you? This is the best treat I have been given since Sorrowful first took me to the Preakness. I promise, sir, I promise that I will name my first son after you."

"My dear, girl," I admonished her. "I do not care at all if you were to have ten sons and name every one of them John Hamish, just please, I beg you, do not lose."

I had heard nothing that day from Holmes. I sent him a note concerning the gambling event and fully expected him to summon me and deliver a severe tongue-lashing for meddling with his client. Instead, I received a note that simply read:

```
Jolly good work, Watson. Regret I cannot
attend. Holmes.
```

Mary and I met Miss Martha the following day for lunch at the Metropole. Her friends, Sorrowful and the chap in the blue suit were with her. I was still awfully worried.

"Martha, my dear," I started in. "You grew up playing poker. But what about this demand that you alternate with whist? Surely that must concern you."

She reached forward and placed her slender hand on my forearm. "*Au contraire,* my friend. For whist, you need to know a hundred rules and remember every card that has been played. All you need to win is a perfect memory. And, well, fortunately, I have one."

She giggled and sat back.

"My dear," I would not let up. "I am no gambler, but I know enough that no matter how good you are, as they say, a good deal depends upon a good deal. Luck still plays a very big role, and even a perfect memory will not overcome it."

"Oh Doctor Watson," she said, warmly. "Luck matters in a short game, but not in an all-nighter."

I was befuddled and asked her to explain.

"The more hands you play, the more that every player will end up being dealt the same quality of cards. It all averages out over time. The scientists call it regression to the mean. That's why I never agree to play in any game under three hours. By the end of a twelve-hour marathon, it is all about your skill. And so I win."

"Very well now, Martha," said my wife. "What then can we do to help? Perhaps a bit of brandy from time to time?"

"No!" interrupted Sorrowful. "No booze. Booze is for losers."

I was somewhat startled by his abrupt comment. Miss Martha explained. "The more a gambler consumes alcohol, the more he loses. I will drink water, some tea and maybe a cup or two of coffee. Sorrowful will be watching everything to make sure that no one tries to slip me a mickey."

"You don't mean," said my wife in disbelief, "that you think someone might try to drug you while you are playing, do you?"

121

"Why not?" said Sorrowful. "Sorry, lady, but you must believe us when we tell you that it is not difficult to do. We know these things."

We parted following lunch. My wife asked Miss Martha concerning her plans for the afternoon and what she planned to do to prepare for the night ahead.

"I am going shopping, having a bath, and a long nap," she replied. Quote a sensible choice, I thought.

Miss Martha's entourage assembled in the St. James Hotel at half-past five o'clock. I had given myself a bit of a disguise, since, by this time in my life, I had become somewhat well-known as a writer and particularly as an associate of Sherlock Holmes. I did not wish for the crowd at Brooks to see me with Miss Martha and make any connection to London's famous detective. It could all too easily scare away possible players.

Martha had spent an hour over in the shops on Regent Street and was now attired in a beautiful little black dress. It barely reached past her knees, had no sleeves, and a very deep and daring cut down the front, exposing the all-American cleavage. Over it she had a short white satin jacket, and around her neck was a fine gold chain, supporting a finely carved gold cross that bobbed up and down each time she moved her head.

"My dear," I said in admiration. "You look positively daring."

"If what you are truly telling me, Doctor, is that I look irresistibly distracting, then I shall take that as assurance that I have accomplished my first task of the night."

We all gave a pleasant chuckle and made our way around the corner to Brooks. The General Secretary was waiting for us and beaming with delight as we entered. He escorted our little troop through the premises to the annex at the back of the building, chatting as he did so.

"I must say," he said, "telegrams were flying all afternoon across the Atlantic. Young lady, you have a bit of a reputation among gamblers. A few of the more dour chaps here have declined to participate as a result but will most certainly be watching. However, we have had over fifty sign up to play, and I had to double the entry fee for those who wished to be first in the queue. We are expecting a positively smashing evening."

Sorrowful had managed to obtain a very respectable set of evening clothes, and Miss Martha entered the annex room on his arm. There must have been over two hundred guests waiting for her, and they stood and gave a round of applause as she gracefully strode into the room. With her high heels, she was more than somewhat taller than most of the men in the room. The Secretary led her to her chair and called the event to order.

After a few perfunctory remarks of welcome, he paused, waiting for complete silence in the room.

"There have been some questions raised concerning the authenticity of our visiting American Girl. I am pleased to confirm that she has placed on deposit with the Club £75,000 and has made it abundantly clear that she will not leave the table until either she has lost her entire deposit or the sun rises."

There were a few gasps from the ladies present and another round of very respectful applause. The Secretary continued.

"The games to be played will alternate between twenty minutes of five-card draw poker and twenty of diminishing contract whist. Hoyle's rules will be followed. Six men at a time will be seated at the table. All will participate in the rounds of poker. Three at a time will play a round of whist, taking turns each time. A player may fold and leave the table at any time. Once a player is the losing player at the table for five rounds of either whist or poker, he must vacate his place and let the next man in the queue take his chair. A five-minute break for the loo will be allowed every hour. A half-hour break for nourishment will take place at midnight. The players may smoke or drink at the table but may not consume food. Guests may, of course, eat and drink as they wish, and our chef has prepared a splendid buffet of delicacies. Are there any questions? No? Very well, let the play begin."

Without any further explanation, he unsealed a deck of cards and placed them in front of one of the men at the table. I recognized him as Hugh Grosvenor, the Duke of Westminster, the bluest of the blue bloods at the table and one of the two richest men in England, if not the world. He was well-known for betting over £100,000 in an evening, losing that much one night, and gaining it back the next. Across from him was his competitor for the title of the wealthiest, Nathan Rothschild, the first Jewish peer in the Empire. The others were all titled men; dukes, an earl, and a marquess.

Most of the men had a snifter of brandy sitting in front of them that was regularly topped up by their valets. With a bit of a flourish, the American chap in the blue suit uncorked a large bottle of Jack Daniels and placed it beside Miss Martha. She tipped it up to her lips and took a small gulp. I was glaring at the chap when he slipped back to his place beside me. He leaned over and whispered in my ear. "Relax, Doc. It's iced tea."

Chapter Twelve

Place Your Bets

uring the first hour of play, the game went back and forth. One chap, who was already well into his cups before the game started and had been swilling more brandy with each set, passed the mark for losing rounds and had to give up his seat. He was replaced by an eager looking young viscount. A few of the players engaged in friendly chit-chat and attempted to draw Miss Martha into conversation. She smiled and provided cryptic one-word answers.

At one point during the second hour, Miss Martha was down by at least twenty thousand, and I had again begun to worry. That concern was quickly vanquished when she raked in an enormous pot in a round of poker and ended up a thousand to the good. By the ten o'clock break, she had slowly but surely increased her lead over everyone else at the table. Several other fellows had been eliminated and replaced, but there were some who were clearly very skilled players, who were not drinking or smoking, and who were also well ahead on the evening.

As the players returned to their chairs, all were seated except for Nathan Rothschild. He stood behind his chair and looked directly at Miss Martha.

"Young lady," he said to her. "I do not know who you are, and you are altogether too beautiful to be the devil incarnate, but you are simply not human. In the past four hours, you have not made a single mistake, you have finessed us relentlessly, not forgotten a single card that has been played, called every one of our bluffs, and bluffed every one of us without pity. While it is not at all sporting on my part, I did not arrive at my station in life by not knowing when to cut my losses. So I will give up my place and wish you good luck, which I am quite certain is the last thing you need."

With the crowd murmuring, he stepped back and sat down among the spectators. He was replaced by another chap, a Mr. Fitzroy Simpson, the first player who bore no title but who was the principal owner of several railways and known to squander vast sums upon the turf.

The turnover in players was now happening more often. As they departed, they left their losings on the table. The bets were steadily increasing in amounts, the pots had reached well over £15,000 a hand, and the tension in the room was palpable. There was no conversation among the players, although there was a constant quiet buzz in the room as the spectators followed the increasing stakes. Occasionally they gave a round of applause when someone, most often Miss Martha, pulled off a daring bluff or finesse. As the midnight hour approached, the room had become rather hot and stuffy, and two of the players removed their suit jackets and vests and played in their shirt sleeves.

"Oh," said Miss Martha. "Good idea. I'm going to join you. She unclasped and removed her white satin jacket and handed it to my wife. She was now sitting upright, her bare shoulders and abundant cleavage fully exposed and disrupting the concentration of her opponents. By the end of the second hour past midnight, she must have been up by over fifty thousand pounds. The railway magnate had lost his limit and graciously gave up his chair, paying some sincere compliments to Miss Martha as he did so. His place was taken by a short, somewhat chubby chap who I recognized immediately. It was Baron Julian, Lord Biggleswade, and he had, as Atherstone had predicted, become heavier and balding.

He was introduced and smiled at the spectators and the rest of the table. "A pleasure to be part of this event and, on behalf of the members of Boodles, my appreciation for opening this event to gentlemen from all the finer clubs. And it is a particular joy to be playing across from such a pretty young filly. Of course, we all know what stallions like to do to fillies."

This off-color comment was met by some nervous guffaws from some of the gentlemen present, and huffs of disapproval from some of the ladies.

Miss Martha looked at the speaker, and a glowing smile spread over her face. "And is that what you do to your fillies, Big Julie?" Again, the men laughed, and the ladies gave her a round of applause. Baron Julian's face turned red, and he stared as his cards.

Over the next hour, the tension continued to grow. A large poker pot was won by Baron Julian. As he gathered his chips, he could not resist gloating. "A shame you lost, Miss. Were you having trouble seeing your cards past your gorgeous big tits?"

Again, some men chuckled at the vulgarity. The rest of the crowd looked at each other in embarrassed silence. Miss Martha smiled very sweetly at the Baron and replied, "Oh, sir. You should see how big they get when I am with company I find exciting." Several of the men present uttered a large "Ha," and some of the ladies giggled. Again, the Baron's face turned red.

To my surprise, Miss Martha appeared to be making some very uncharacteristic mistakes. Over the next thirty minutes, she dropped at least £15,000, mostly in hands won by Baron Julian. I gave a concerned glance to Sorrowful, who winked back at me. In the hand before the break, the Baron won again, and this time, he raked in close to £8000. Miss Martha was looking very flustered and reached for her bottle of Jack Daniels. The players rose from their chairs and stepped back to chat with their colleagues, or enjoy a cigarette, or made a beeline to the loo.

The Baron walked over to where Miss Martha was sitting and leaned over her shoulder.

"My dear little girl," he said. "When you get to the loo, you better unload some of your whiskey."

She looked angrily back at him and snapped, "And while you're there, why don't you shake hands with shorty?" He raised his hand as if he were about to strike her and was immediately grabbed and restrained by the chap beside him. Miss Martha smiled in feigned sweetness and came over to where her friends were sitting.

"My dear," said my wife, "are you quite all right? Do you need to get some air? That rude man is getting to you."

Miss Martha smiled and giggled. "When a player has to use insults and rudeness to distract you, it is a sure sign he is a loser. Any minute now, he will try to cheat. Just you watch."

So watch we did. There only two original players remaining at the table were Hugh Grosvenor and Miss Martha. The Duke of Westminster was down at least £100,000 but had avoided losing enough rounds to be removed from the table, and no one doubted that he could lose another million and not miss it. The Baron won several more hands and continued to direct rude and condescending insults at Miss Martha. She continued to smile.

Sunrise would arrive just before 5:00 am. We had entered the final hour of play. Miss Martha was still up well over £50,000 but had lost money on several of the last rounds, both in whist and poker. At 4:30 am, it was her turn as dealer in a round of five-card draw. She dealt the cards and responded to the draw requests from three of the players, including Baron Julian. She drew none herself.

"Getting a bit overconfident, are we Miss?" teased Baron Julian. "Not a good sign."

The first player was Hugh Grosvenor. Instead of sliding in the agreed-upon ante, he smiled at the other players and said, "Not much time left. I say we make this a little more interesting. What say we up the ante to £10,000?" The crowd gasped. The Duke had been known to make calls like this in a long game to, as he said, "separate the men from the boys." Everyone nodded, all either too confident in the hands they held or too proud not to go along. The piles of chips were moved into the pot. Grosvenor then led off the bids.

"I will bet £20,000," he said, keeping his face deliberately blank. Again, the crowd gasped. They all knew that they were observing the richest round of cards that had ever been seen in London. The next two players matched his bid but did not raise it. Baron Julian smiled and slid forward his £20,000 and boldly announced a raise of another £10,000. The fifth chap, who was known to be a very astute player, laid down his cards and folded. Now it was up to Miss Martha.

"Okay. £30,000 it is."

Murmurs of wonder swept the room, and a small round of applause was given. Now the bid passed to Grosvenor. He raised another £10,000 and slid £40,000 into the center of the table. The next two fellows laid down their cards and folded, obviously smart enough to know when to stop losing a fortune. The Baron met the bid but did not raise. The final bid went to Miss Martha, who also met the bid.

"I believe it is showdown time," Miss Martha said with a smile, looking over to Hugh Grosvenor.

He laughed and said, "I really have nothing at all. I just thought we needed a little more excitement." He laid his cards on the table, showing three Kings. It was, in truth, not a bad hand, and we all wondered what the other two must be holding.

Lord Biggleswade smiled a triumphal smile. "Lady Luck has been smiling on me. It does not get much better, now does it?"

With a hand flourish for each card he laid on the table, he showed four Aces and a King of Diamonds. He began to reach forward to gather the chips.

"Uh, uh. Not so fast, my good man," said the Duke. "Miss. Your hand, please."

Miss Martha shrugged and, one at a time, laid her cards down. The first was a two of spades, one of the weakest cards in a deck. It was followed by the three of spades, which was, in turn, followed by the four. She paused and looked at the crowd with a grin spreading across her face. The entire room stopped breathing. She then laid down the five. She held the last card close to her chest and then slowly placed the ace of spades on the table. A straight flush. The second highest hand in poker. The pot was hers. The crowd erupted into cheers and applause. Over £100,000 was moved across the table toward her. Hugh Grosvenor was beaming at her.

"Well done, my dear. Well done. Bravely played, indeed," he enthused.

The other two players reached across the table and shook her hand in congratulations.

"Sit down," barked the baron. "The night is not over. There is still time for two more hands. Your Lordship, I believe you are the dealer. Pray proceed."

As the Duke began to shuffle the cards, the General Secretary of Brooks leaned his head down to the ear of the baron. I watched as his eyes went wide and his face reddened. Without a word, he rose from his chair, turned, and walked out of the room.

I was very confused and leaned over to the chap beside me. "What was that all about?"

He whispered back, "Biggleswade is not a member at Brooks, so he had no account here. He can only play to the limit of his deposit. He must have passed that mark on the last round. So, he has to drop out. Those are the rules."

130

There was murmuring throughout the room. Sunrise would come in less than ten minutes. Hugh Grosvenor, the Duke of Westminster, stood and addressed all of the guests.

"Ladies and gentlemen, as there is not sufficient time for another full round, may I suggest that we declare the game over and give our congratulations to this exceptional young woman."

A roar of applause and hurrahs went up. The Duke continued. "I do believe that a round of Champagne is called for. And some breakfast."

Several of the younger women came forward to congratulate Miss Martha. She responded graciously and invited them all to visit her in New York. About half an hour later, we made our way out of the club and onto the sidewalk.

"Good heavens," said my wife. "How much did you win? Your parents will be very thrilled when they hear about it."

A look of fear came over the young woman's pretty face. "Oh no. You can't let them know. My mom would have fifty fits."

Chapter Thirteen

Real Gamblers Don't Cry

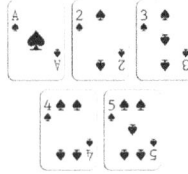

Having had enough nail-biting excitement, my wife, Mary, and I took Miss Martha to Kew Gardens and the Tower of London. She enjoyed it, or, at least, she was sufficiently gracious to convince us that she did.

On the third day, Holmes called us all together, and we gathered in Baker Street.

"I was afraid that we might not have a response to our note in *Sporting News*," he said to us. "This morning a message was delivered to the desk at the Metropole providing us with our next step in finding Sir Galahad."

He passed around the note. It ran:

```
Fee £10,000. Cash only. Breeding mare in
heat to be brought to stable near London
next week. Confirm to Sporting News
agony. Galahad.
```

"Good lord," I exclaimed. "£10,000 stud fee. That is unheard of. Preposterous."

"For a horse," said the man in the blue suit, "what can win the Kentucky Derby, it's a bargain. It's a deal, except we need a mare. You got one of those, Mr. Sherlock?"

"As a matter of fact, sir, I do. An excellent one who will be itching to meet a stallion on Monday. With your permission, I shall respond and appear to be most eager. If Sir Galahad is willing, then we, the representatives of an American syndicate, will take our mare for breeding in a few days. You will have to be ready to play your parts. Now excuse me for a few minutes while I draft our reply."

He sat down at the writing desk and picked up his pen. His first two efforts were thrown into the trash, and then he brought the third version to us for our approval.

```
Sir Galahad: Fee confirmed. Estrous on
Tuesday and Wednesday. Please confirm
rendezvous location. Reply to Metropole.
```

"I think that should do the trick," he said. "Watson, would you mind again dropping this off. If it appears in the Sunday paper, that will give us sufficient time to prepare."

"Certainly, Holmes," I replied. "And just where do you plan to find a mare in heat for a Tuesday breeding session?"

"One of the finest in the kingdom," he said with a grin, "will be waiting."

The notice was placed. It appeared on Sunday, and by Monday morning, a reply had been received telling us to be at the North Dulwich Station with the mare at 10:00 am the following day. I could not imagine where Holmes would find a mare in heat and wondered what his alternative plan was. However, I dutifully showed up at Baker Street at 7:00 am on Tuesday morning, dressed in a dark suit and wearing gold-rimmed glasses, and trying to look very much like an American accountant.

Holmes was waiting for me. He was wearing an American-cut suit jacket with a design of Royal Stewart tartan and tan trousers. He had one of his favorite wigs on his head, covered by a fedora hat. I thought it quite comical and suggested that he could secure employment as a warning post to divert traffic. He did not appear to find this amusing. While we were standing in the front room, another man, not one of the Americans, came down the hall from the bedroom that had once been mine. His suit jacket was a bright red and black check with matching trousers. He had a Bowler hat on his head, thick dark-rimmed glasses and a handlebar mustache. He was somewhat shorter than I and had a narrow, pointed face. I kept looking at this fellow for nearly a minute before I exploded in laughter and fell back onto the sofa.

"Enough, Watson," shouted Inspector Lestrade of Scotland Yard. "You will act with respect even if I am wearing a ridiculous costume."

I bit my lip and stood up again. "Inspector," I said, "always good to see you again." But then I could not help myself, and I started to laugh again. I thought he was going to take a few strips off my hide but, fortunately, laughter is contagious, and he was soon laughing along with me. Even Holmes joined in.

"I have never," I sputtered, "seen three Englishmen looking so ridiculous."

"We are looking," said Holmes, "like three gentlemen from America who are involved in the sport of horse racing."

"Same thing," said Lestrade, and we laughed some more.

"And where, might I ask," I asked, "are the real Americans?"

"They are meeting us in Herne Hill in an hour, along with our lovely heated mare."

We endured the gawking and stares of the passengers as we took the short hop from Victoria Station south to Herne Hill. We were met at the station by Miss Martha, Sorrowful, and the chap in the blue suit. They were standing beside a fine-looking horse trailer, attached to a small motorized tractor. I could see the trailer wobbling from time to time as its passenger shifted herself around inside. Miss Martha rushed up to us.

"Mr. Holmes. She's beautiful. Where did you find her? She has to be the most perfect mare I have ever seen. She's just like Black Beauty. Can we call her Black Beauty?"

"Most certainly," said Holmes, clearly pleased with himself. He opened the top of the Dutch door on the back of the trailer, and I observed a gleaming black back end of a large mare. She was pawing and whining and letting us know that she was not altogether happy.

"Very well, Holmes," I said. "Where in heaven's name did you find her?"

"I had some help."

"Mycroft, no doubt," I said.

"Precisely."

"Mycroft does not own any horses."

"He has friends who do."

It then struck me. "Did that mare come down from Sandringham?"

"Yes. I believe that Black Beauty was from Norfolk. Is that not correct, Miss Martha?"

"That is true," the young woman replied.

"Holmes," I said in disbelief. "You cannot possibly be saying that you brought one of the King's horses to be part of your masquerade."

"He has rather a lot of them. He shan't miss one mare for the day."

Sorrowful drove the tractor, and the remaining five of us walked along beside it down Half Moon Lane and over to the North Dulwich Station. We arrived at the rendezvous location at ten

135

minutes before ten and waited for someone to come and meet us. At ten minutes past the hour, a large four-wheeler approached from the south. It was a fine-looking vehicle, drawn by two mares, also fine-looking. On the driver's seat were two young men, both in a military type of uniform, but one that I did not recognize. They stepped down and came over to us. A third chap emerged from inside the carriage. All were tall and quite athletic, and by their walk, I guessed that they had seen time in the service.

The chap in the blue suit extended his hand toward them. "A pleasure to meet you, gentlemen. Allow me to introduce ..."

He got no further, and no hand was given to his in response. One of the young men bluntly interrupted him and said, "Introductions are neither necessary nor wanted. Your identity will remain unknown to us as will ours to you. It is better that way. Please confirm that you have the funds required."

Lestrade reached into his pocket and produced a large wad of hundred-pound notes. One of the fellows took it, counted it, nodded, and handed the money back.

I had not expected quite this type of chilly reception, and what came next was even more off-putting. The fellow who had been in the carriage reached into a satchel and pulled out an armful of black velvet cloth. I could see that there were several individual items in the bundle. He extracted a cloth bag with a drawstring attached to the top and handed it to me. Then he gave one to each of the others.

"Please enter the carriage and then place these over your heads and draw the cords tight. I will check them once you are in your seats. Do not ask any questions."

We all glanced over to Holmes, who gave a small nod, and we did as instructed. We entered the carriage. It was large enough for all of us to have a seat. The third chap made sure all of the cloth bags were securely over our heads and tied before he sat down on the floor.

We could hear one of our captors climb up onto the driver's seat and the other one starting the tractor.

For the next half hour, we clattered along at a slow pace, no faster than a tractor pulling a horse trailer could do safely. We came to a stop, and I heard the driver jump down and then heard a gate swing open. The carriage drove through the gate, and then it was closed. About two minutes later, we came to a halt.

"Gentlemen and lady," said the chap inside the carriage, "Please remove your masks and leave the carriage."

Again, we did as instructed, and I could see that we were on the grounds of a small stable operation. It had one barn and three paddocks. The open fields could not have been much more than ten acres. A neat little red-brick villa with overhanging eaves stood on the far side of the lane.

"Lead your mare into the paddock," ordered the fellow who had been driving the tractor. Sorrowful and the chap in the blue suit opened the side door of the trailer, dropped the ramp, and led the gleaming raven-black mare toward the paddock. On seeing her, the fellow who had given the order let out a low whistle of admiration.

"Crikey, she is a beauty. And you brought her all the way from New York? Her colts will be the fastest things on this planet."

"Quiet!" shouted the fellow who had been in the carriage. It was clear that they were under orders not to speak beyond the absolute minimum.

"Wait here," the same fellow ordered. "We will bring the stallion."

He walked toward the barn, leaving our little troop alone to chat privately for the first time.

"Well now, welcome to merry old England," said the chap in the blue suit. "Anybody have any idea where we are?"

"Not the foggiest," said Lestrade.

I had an inkling that Holmes would not give the same answer.

"Where are we, Holmes?" I asked.

"We turned into a lane off of Croxted Road, one and a quarter miles south of the village square."

"And just how is it, Mr. Sherlock-the-Detective, that you know that seeing as how you are not seeing all the way here?"

"Elementary. The carriage wheels have a diameter of four feet, giving them a circumference of close to twelve and a half feet. The right rear wheel has a dent in it that creates a very small bump with every rotation. All you have to do is count the humps, multiply by the circumference, and you know your distance."

"And you are doing this all the way from there to here? Counting every bump?"

"Of course not. It was only necessary to count for the first few estimated minutes, which I believe you could also judge quite accurately, given your years of watching them pass at a racetrack. Then you time the bumps per minute. As soon as our masks came off, I looked at my watch and knew how many minutes we had been traveling. I believe it is called doing arithmetic."

Given her penchant for numbers, I was sure that Miss Martha was about to interrogate Holmes further, but any conversation was cut short by the emergence of the stallion, Sir Galahad, from the barn. He was led by a fierce-looking and gnarly older man, and a strikingly handsome young groom. And, my goodness, but Sir Galahad was an enormous horse; I guessed at least eighteen hands tall, with a large, powerful chest and massive legs. His coloring was piebald, with alternating large blotches of black and white, something akin to a Holstein cow.

"Oh my," gasped Miss Martha. "He is a big fellow. *Sir* Galahad, indeed."

Chapter Fourteen

The Claiming

The older fellow and the groom led him into the paddock where Black Beauty was prancing around in apparent eager expectation. Sir Galahad had picked up the scent, and the men moved quickly to open the paddock gate and let him inside before he kicked it down. While we were moving toward the fence of the paddock, Holmes made a small detour to the door of the stable, where he bent down and picked up a pail, and then carried it back to our vantage point. Odd, I thought.

We stood and watched a scene that is familiar to all people who have lived on farms and foreign to city folk. For a few minutes, both horses galloped around the paddock, seeming to ignore each other. Then Black Beauty stood still, and Sir Galahad approached her slowly. He lowered his great head and neck and brought his muzzle alongside hers and gently rubbed. Twice she jumped back and feigned a nip at him. He startled and backed off and then approached again, this time running his muzzle along her spine as if grooming her. After a few minutes of that, he was sniffing at her haunches and then, in a quick movement, mounted her. She just stood still and appeared indifferent to the entire event. In less than half a minute, he was off of her and back alongside, his large face rubbing up against hers, the equine equivalent of afterglow. Then the big fellow trotted around the paddock for a minute or two before the elderly chap, and the groom brought him back to the gate.

"Well now," came a voice from behind us. "Did you enjoy watching that? No doubt, little girl, it made you even randier than you already were."

I turned around and recognized Baron Julian. I assume that he had been waiting in the small cottage behind us.

"How delightful," he continued, "that the little trollop who took my money is now paying me back, one breeding session at a time."

Miss Martha smiled. "Nice stallion. Oh … I was speaking about the horse, not you, short stuff."

I could see the anger flash in his eyes, but he controlled himself and smiled. "It is always a pleasure to serve a pretty young customer, even if she has poor manners. I look forward to your next visit with another mare. And because I am sure that my horse likes you even less than I do, the fee will have to go up to £12,000." He smiled again, smugly.

"I dare say," said Holmes, ignoring the exchange that was taking place. "This big fellow looks a bit overheated after such strenuous exertion. Mr. Sorrowful, would you mind holding him here for just a moment while I help him to cool down?"

Sorrowful looked perplexed but came up and held the tether rope while Holmes reached into the pail and lifted out a washing sponge, dripping with water. He walked up to the side of Sir Galahad and began to rub his flank with the sponge.

"Get your hands off of my horse!" shouted Lord Biggleswade. "Stop that. Stop it now!" He began to walk quickly toward Holmes and the horse.

Holmes looked over at the chap in the blue suit and me and said, "Gentlemen, please restrain the young lord. This poor fellow needs a bath."

I had no idea what in the world Holmes was up to, but I immediately put my body in front of the angry young lord. The fellow in the blue suit did the same, except he put his face less than two inches from the baron's and said, "Mr. Lordy Dordy, I am not a man of violence. Therefore, I request that you abide by the instructions, or else we shall have to settle our difference somewhat less than amiably."

"Stop this instant!" came the reply. He was now screaming at Holmes.

"Ladies and gentlemen," said Holmes, smiling from ear to ear. "Allow me to introduce you to Mr. Silver."

Sorrowful pulled the stallion around so that we could see his flank. Half of the large black patch that had been there had vanished. I was thunderstruck. We all stood and stared in disbelief. The black and white piebald coloring was dripping away before our eyes.

"If we keep giving this big boy a good scrubbing, he will come out white as snow all over. It appears he was never in a fire at all. And there, my friends," he said, pointing at the baron, "is the horse thief and the man who murdered Colonel Ross's trainer and groom and most likely his own jockey."

The young lord issued a string of cursing at Holmes, of which I can interpret as his denying everything and telling us to go to the devil.

"Lies! Infernal lies. You have not a shred of evidence for that slander," he shouted. "I will have you sued until you are bankrupt and unfit for decent society."

The stooped over elderly trainer stepped forward. "You won't need evidence. I will testify. He killed them, and I helped him."

"Ah, Mr. Silas Brown, I presume," said Holmes.

"I am," said the old man.

"Brown!" shouted the Baron. "You will keep your mouth shut if you know what's good for you!"

"I know," Brown said to Holmes, "what is good for me. I know I have cancer, and it will not be long before I stand before God and have to account for myself. And I am not going to die with this on my conscience. His lordship and I stole Mr. Silver and replaced him with a big old white stallion from his stable. Then we knocked the two fellows out with a blackjack and put them in the stall. I will confess to that. But I swear I did not know he was going to burn the place down. I swear I did not."

The look on the baron's face had turned to wide-eyed panic. In a quick few steps, he rushed up to Miss Martha and grabbed her around the neck with his forearm. Out of his pocket, he pulled a small revolver and placed its barrel against her temple.

"Get this straight!" he commanded. "Every one of you get back into the carriage and off of this property. And then get out of England. This little …" He used a term more properly applied to a female dog. "… is going to stay here with me until you are gone. Gone! Forever! GET OUT!"

At this point, Lestrade removed his Bowler hat, peeled off his mustache, and doffed his ridiculous suit jacket, exposing a vest emblazoned with the crest of the Scotland Yard.

"Your lordship," he said calmly, "you are already in enough trouble, and it would be best if you stopped now and came with me and we can have a bit of a chat back in London. You might wish to call your barrister. That is quite acceptable."

"I don't believe you!" came the angered reply. "Now get out of here, or I will kill her. Do you understand? I will kill her!"

Miss Martha gave a wink that the baron could not see. She held her hand closely in front of her stomach and exposed three fingers. She closed her fist and then extended first one finger, then two. An instant later, she kicked both her legs forward, and her body dropped like a stone onto the ground. She had not even hit the gravel before a gun beside me exploded, and I saw the baron twist violently. His revolver flew from his hand, and he fell to the ground clutching his shoulder.

"We used to practice that," said Sorrowful, "when she was a kid. Never knew it would come in handy." He put his revolver back into his pocket.

Lestrade was bending over the baron. "Dr. Watson, please help me get this fellow back into the cottage and bandaged up. I cannot tell from here, but the wound does not look overly serious. There is a wire coming out of the cottage, and I will wager he has a telephone service … Come now, your lordship. Up you get. Come along now."

The baron struggled to his feet, cursing while doing so. As Lestrade led him away, he turned back and shouted at us, "I have the best barrister in the country. I will be back in two days, and I am coming after you. And you," he said, looking at Martha, "when I get back, I am going to do exactly what that stallion did."

"Lovely," she shouted back. "I can't wait. I'll have the mare waiting for you."

It was not long before a police wagon, and two constables arrived from the village. The baron's wound was minor, and I had bandaged it up adequately until he could be taken under police guard to the local hospital. Lestrade left the baron in the constables' care, and we commandeered the large carriage that had brought us. Holmes and I found the three chaps who had met us at the station, sitting in their guardhouse playing cards, laughing loudly and oblivious to what had occurred in the stable area.

Holmes had removed his hat, wig, eyebrows, side-whiskers, mustache and silly jacket. He approached the startled guards.

"Terribly sorry to bother you chaps, but as your employer is on his way to prison and maybe even the gallows, I wonder if one of you might be willing to drive us back to the Paxton pub. It is just a mile or so up to the right from your gate; about halfway to the village square."

The guards were bright enough to remember that Holmes and all the rest of us had been hooded on the way here and looked at him in bewilderment.

"Who in the devil's name are *you*?" said the one who had been sitting on the floor.

"I am Sherlock Holmes," he said. "And I might add that Chief Inspector Lestrade will be one of your passengers. He was quite impressed with the way you carried out your assignment on the way here. I recommend you ask him about employment opportunities with the police."

The look on their faces was rather amusing. One of them was bright enough to jump to his feet, straighten his uniform and respond, "Right away, sir. Happy to oblige. The carriage is this way. Please, sir. Does the lady require any assistance?"

Chapter Fifteen

Winning the Cup

An hour later. our motley crew was gathered in Paxton's Pub in West Dulwich, enjoying various libations and some excellent meat pies.

"What," asked Miss Martha, "are you going to do with Black Beauty? You can't just leave her there."

Holmes nodded. "I asked Mr. Silas Brown and the groom if they would look after returning her to her home stable, and they have agreed to do so. She will be well looked after."

"My goodness," I exclaimed. "You are sending those two up to Sandringham? To the King's stables? That would give them a bit of a thrill, I'll warrant."

"For a brief moment," said Holmes, "they thought I was sending them to New York, and so Norfolk came as a bit of a disappointment. And who knows, but perhaps they will find employment up there."

We chuckled at the thought and at the fleeting prospect of accompanying a mare back across the Atlantic.

"Very well now, Holmes," said Lestrade. He was acting a bit on the sour side as always, but I was quite sure he was pleased as punch with the prospect of arresting a member of the nobility, booking a triple murder, and returning a prize racehorse to its rightful owner. "Very well, now. Out with it. How in the devil did you sort it all out? I know you are dying to tell me."

"Am I now?" replied Holmes coolly. Then he smiled, "Ah, my dear inspector, you have come to know me all too well. I will confess that it was one of the more perplexing cases I have had to solve and a most distressing one as well. I am terribly disappointed that it took five years. But here it goes. The presence of foul play in the deaths of Baron Julian's jockey and Colonel Ross's groom and trainer was obvious. I confess that I first suspected the colonel as he, at least, had the motive of benefitting from the very large insurance settlement. I must thank my dear friend, Dr. Watson, for disabusing me of that notion. The Americans had only a weak and remote motive, and I could not ascribe to Mr. Harry-the-Horse the ability to be so utterly convincing an actor. His emotional, indeed passionate response to the events that had taken place were entirely convincing.

"As to Lord Atherstone, again, there was simply no motive. He already has more money than God and would consign his precious soul to hell should he ever transgress one jot or tittle of the rules of the Jockey Club. That left Baron Julian. I will fully acknowledge that I am of the curmudgeonly opinion that old money should not jingle, and I do not hold in high regard those pretentious young men who seek to make a show of their family wealth. He was clearly spending money like it was water, but there was no report of his ever being short of it.

"Clearly the most lucrative years of a winning racehorse are the years when he is put out to stud. And I kept looking through the *Sporting News* for any reference to any of the other horses from that race that ended in the money, or even the also-rans, to see if they were receiving outrageous fees for their siring service. None was, and of course, I was looking for the wrong horse.

"It was not until Miss Martha mentioned the high ratio of white offspring of the mysterious Sir Galahad that the light dawned upon me. If there were that many offspring that were white, then the sire must be white. There was no reference in the *Sporting News* to any highly exceptional white racehorse in the past ten years that was white, except for Mr. Silver. Added to that was Miss Martha's information that the normal ratio was about two in a hundred. That meant that, while rare, white horses are still to be found. Given the number of horses bred in a large stable, the possibility of some stables having another massive white stallion could not be eliminated.

"The alacrity with which our notice in the agony column was responded to indicated that whoever we were dealing with was eager to increase his flow of cash, and that tipped the scales slightly toward the young baron. On arriving at his place in Dulwich, I was still not entirely sure until I saw the young groom who was with Mr. Silas Brown.

"You recognized him?" I said in amazement.

"Yes, my dear doctor, and although I know you will not take kindly to my saying so, so should have you. He was standing by one of the stalls in the baron's stable when we visited them in the Cotswolds five years ago, and he was wearing the same style of skin-tight jodhpurs.

"Even having deduced that Lord Biggleswade was the villain, it would still have been difficult to tie him directly to the events of five years ago had it not been for the delightful gambling tournament at Brooks."

He paused and looked around at the group of us.

"I am afraid, Mr. Sherlock the Detective," said the chap in the blue suit, "that you are going to have to explain that one on account of because I do not see any connection whatsoever except that he is too dumb to know when he is beat."

"Baron Julian could have remained unseen in the cottage. Once he observed my cleaning Mr. Silver, he could have slipped away without our apprehending him. I am quite certain, given the secrecy with which he kept the small stable in Dulwich, that his name appears nowhere on the deeds or ownership and that any rents are paid anonymously through third parties. But when he saw the young lady who had trounced him at cards a few days ago, he could not resist making himself known and treating Miss Martha like a suppliant. His pride got the better of him and led to his being exposed. He will likely have hung himself."

"But why," asked Lestrade, "the murders?"

"Colonel Ross's trainer and groom had spent the past four years every day caring for Mr. Silver. They would have known immediately that the braised carcass of the horse in the stall was not theirs. As to murdering his own jockey, I suspect that he may have tried to have the poor fellow become part of the plan and was refused, but that is merely conjecture. I shall have to leave that to you, my dear inspector, to glean that information."

Lestrade nodded. "Not a bad little business he had going. Over a hundred stud fees collected at £10,000 a round. Not a bad business at all. Or was it more?"

"Far more," said Holmes. "that was only for mares brought from America. He was also servicing mares from India, Japan, Canada, the RSA, and the Antipodes. The big fellow was generating utter boatloads of income. All in cash. It was a very good business."

"Very well, Holmes," said Lestrade as he rose from his place at the table. "Your methods are beyond my imagination, but you have done it again. However, we really must give credit where it is due. This young lady has been quite surprisingly talented and resourceful. I will have a citation drawn up and sent to her family, commending her courage and her service to Scotland Yard."

He smiled down at Miss Martha. To his surprise, she recoiled in fear.

"Oh please, Inspector Lestrade. Please do not do that. If my mom found out what I've been up to, she'd have fifty fits."

Did you enjoy this story? Are there ways it could have been improved? Please help the author and future readers of future New Sherlock Holmes Mysteries by posting a review on the site from which you purchased this book. Thanks, and happy sleuthing and deducing.

Dear Sherlockian Reader:

When you are raised, as I was, in a conservative Christian home, horse races and related betting reside on another planet. I confess that my very first visit to a racetrack in my entire life took place in July of 2014 when we attended the Silver Blaze Event at the Woodbine Racetrack in Toronto, hosted by the Bootmakers.

Since then, I have not become a regular attendee but I have read and learned a lot about *The Sport of Kings*.

As a result, the references in this story to racetracks and to various cup and stakes race are more or less accurate for the years 1899 through 1905. The *Race of the Century* is fictional. Names of race horses and jockeys are inspired by the names of real ones past and present.

The calling of the Wheatcroft Cup Race was adapted with only a few additions from the transcript of one of the greatest horse races of modern times – the winning of the 1973 Belmont by *Secretariat*, by an unheard of thirty-one lengths. That thrilling race can be seen on YouTube and is well worth watching.

Readers who are far better acquainted with the Sport of Kings than I are encouraged to contact me so I can correct or improve any of the content related to horse racing.

The Brooks Club on St. James is wonderfully famous for the reasons described. Most of the characters who are noted as members in 1906 were indeed there at that time. This includes Sir Edward Bulwer-Lytton, the prolific author of many popular novels of their day including *Paul Clifford*, a book whose plot and contents are totally forgettable and whose opening sentence is immortal.

Queen Victoria was monarch of Great Britain from 1837 through 1901, succeeded by her son 'Bertie' better known as Edward VII. She was a great fan of horse racing, as is her great-great-granddaughter.

There are numerous other tributes and references – *Easter eggs* – scattered through the story with the hope that they will add to the readers' enjoyment.

Thank you for reading this story. Hope you enjoyed it.

Warm regards,

Craig

About the Author

In May of 2014 the Sherlock Holmes Society of Canada – better known as The Bootmakers (www.torontobootmakers.com) – announced a contest for a new Sherlock Holmes story. Although he had no experience writing fiction, the author submitted a short Sherlock Holmes mystery and was blessed to be declared one of the winners. Thus inspired, he has continued to write new Sherlock Holmes mysteries since. He has been writing these stories while living in Toronto, Tokyo, Manhattan, Bahrain, Buenos Aires and the Okanagan Valley.

New Sherlock Holmes Mysteries
by Craig Stephen Copland

www.SherlockHolmesMystery.com

"Best selling series of new Sherlock Holmes stories. All faithful to The Canon."

This is the first book in the series. Go to my website, start with this one and enjoy MORE SHERLOCK.

Studying Scarlet. Starlet O'Halloran, a fabulous mature woman, who reminds the reader of Scarlet O'Hara (but who, for copyright reasons cannot actually be her) has arrived in London looking for her long-lost husband, Brett (who resembles Rhett Butler, but who, for copyright reasons, cannot actually be him). She enlists the help of Sherlock Holmes. This is an unauthorized parody, inspired by Arthur Conan Doyle's *A Study in Scarlet* and Margaret Mitchell's *Gone with the Wind*.

Six new Sherlock Holmes stories are always free to enjoy. If you have not already read them, go to this site, sign up, download and enjoy. www.SherlockHolmesMystery.com

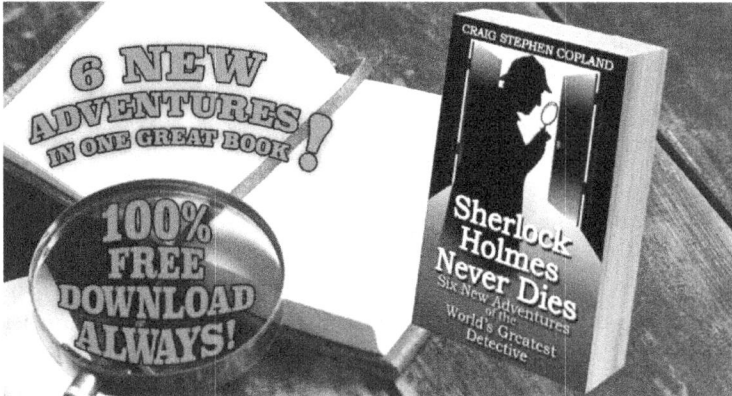

Super Collections A, B and C

57 New Sherlock Holmes Mysteries.

The perfect ebooks for readers who subscribe to Kindle Unlimited

Enter 'Craig Stephen Copland Sherlock Holmes Super Collection' into your Amazon search bar. Enjoy over 2 million words of MORE SHERLOCK.

www.SherlockHolmesMystery.com

The Adventure of Silver Blaze

Silver Blaze

The Original Sherlock Holmes Story

Arthur Conan Doyle

The Adventure of Silver Blaze

"I am afraid, Watson, that I shall have to go," said Holmes, as we sat down together to our breakfast one morning.

"Go! Where to?"

"To Dartmoor; to King's Pyland."

I was not surprised. Indeed, my only wonder was that he had not already been mixed upon this extraordinary case, which was the one topic of conversation through the length and breadth of England. For a whole day my companion had rambled about the room with his chin upon his chest and his brows knitted, charging and recharging his pipe with the strongest black tobacco, and absolutely deaf to any of my questions or remarks. Fresh editions of every paper had been sent up by our news agent, only to be glanced over and tossed down into a corner. Yet, silent as he was, I knew perfectly well what it was over which he was brooding. There was but one problem before the public which could challenge his powers of analysis, and that was the singular disappearance of the favorite for the Wessex Cup, and the tragic murder of its trainer. When, therefore, he suddenly announced his intention of setting out for the scene of the drama it was only what I had both expected and hoped for.

"I should be most happy to go down with you if I should not be in the way," said I.

"My dear Watson, you would confer a great favor upon me by coming. And I think that your time will not be misspent, for there are points about the case which promise to make it an absolutely unique one. We have, I think, just time to catch our train at Paddington, and I will go further into the matter upon our journey. You would oblige me by bringing with you your very excellent field-glass."

And so it happened that an hour or so later I found myself in the corner of a first-class carriage flying along en route for Exeter, while Sherlock Holmes, with his sharp, eager face framed in his ear-flapped travelling-cap, dipped rapidly into the bundle of fresh papers which he had procured at Paddington. We had left Reading far behind us before he thrust the last one of them under the seat, and offered me his cigar-case.

"We are going well," said he, looking out the window and glancing at his watch. "Our rate at present is fifty-three and a half miles an hour."

"I have not observed the quarter-mile posts," said I.

"Nor have I. But the telegraph posts upon this line are sixty yards apart, and the calculation is a simple one. I presume that you have looked into this matter of the murder of John Straker and the disappearance of Silver Blaze?"

"I have seen what the Telegraph and the Chronicle have to say."

"It is one of those cases where the art of the reasoner should be used rather for the sifting of details than for the acquiring of fresh evidence. The tragedy has been so uncommon, so complete and of such personal importance to so many people, that we are suffering from a plethora of surmise, conjecture, and hypothesis. The difficulty is to detach the framework of fact -- of absolute undeniable fact -- from the embellishments of theorists and reporters. Then, having established ourselves upon this sound basis, it is our duty to see what inferences may be drawn and what are the special points upon which the whole mystery turns. On Tuesday evening, I received telegrams from both Colonel Ross, the owner of the horse, and from Inspector Gregory, who is looking after the case, inviting my cooperation.

"Tuesday evening!" I exclaimed. "And this is Thursday morning. Why didn't you go down yesterday?"

"Because I made a blunder, my dear Watson -- which is, I am afraid, a more common occurrence than any one would think who only knew me through your memoirs. The fact is that I could not believe is possible that the most remarkable horse in England could long remain concealed, especially in so sparsely inhabited a place as the north of Dartmoor. From hour to hour yesterday, I expected to hear that he had been found, and that his abductor was the murderer of John Straker. When, however, another morning had come, and I found that beyond the arrest of young Fitzroy Simpson nothing had been done, I felt that it was time for me to take action. Yet in some ways, I feel that yesterday has not been wasted."

"You have formed a theory, then?"

"At least, I have got a grip of the essential facts of the case. I shall enumerate them to you, for nothing clears up a case so much as stating it to another person, and I can hardly expect your co-operation if I do not show you the position from which we start."

I lay back against the cushions, puffing at my cigar, while Holmes, leaning forward, with his long, thin forefinger checking off the points upon the palm of his left hand, gave me a sketch of the events which had led to our journey.

"Silver Blaze," said he, "is from the Somomy stock, and holds as brilliant a record as his famous ancestor. He is now in his fifth year, and has brought in turn each of the prizes of the turf to Colonel

Ross, his fortunate owner. Up to the time of the catastrophe, he was the first favorite for the Wessex Cup, the betting being three to one on him. He has always, however, been a prime favorite with the racing public, and has never yet disappointed them, so that even at those odds enormous sums of money have been laid upon him. It is obvious, therefore, that there were many people who had the strongest interest in preventing Silver Blaze from being there at the fall of the flag next Tuesday.

"The fact was, of course, appreciated at King's Pyland, where the Colonel's training-stable is situated. Every precaution was taken to guard the favorite. The trainer, John Straker, is a retired jockey who rode in Colonel Ross's colors before he became too heavy for the weighing-chair. He has served the Colonel for five years as jockey and for seven as trainer, and has always shown himself to be a zealous and honest servant. Under him were three lads; for the establishment was a small one, containing only four horses in all. One of these lads sat up each night in the stable, while the others slept in the loft. All three bore excellent characters. John Straker, who is a married man, lived in a small villa about two hundred yards from the stables. He has no children, keeps one maid-servant, and is comfortably off. The country round is very lonely, but about half a mile to the north, there is a small cluster of villas which have been built by a Tavistock contractor for the use of invalids and others who may wish to enjoy the pure Dartmoor air. Tavistock itself lies two miles to the west, while across the moor, also about two miles distant, is the larger training establishment of Mapleton, which belongs to Lord Backwater, and is managed by Silas Brown. In every other direction, the moor is a complete wilderness, inhabited only be a few roaming gypsies. Such was the general situation last Monday night when the catastrophe occurred.

"On that evening the horses had been exercised and watered as usual, and the stables were locked up at nine o'clock. Two of the lads walked up to the trainer's house, where they had supper in the kitchen, while the third, Ned Hunter, remained on guard. At a few minutes after nine the maid, Edith Baxter, carried down to the stables his supper, which consisted of a dish of curried mutton. She took no liquid, as there was a water-tap in the stables, and it was the rule that the lad on duty should drink nothing else. The maid carried a lantern with her, as it was very dark and the path ran across the open moor.

"Edith Baxter was within thirty yards of the stables, when a man appeared out of the darkness and called to her to stop. As he stepped into the circle of yellow light thrown by the lantern she saw that he was a person of gentlemanly bearing, dressed in a gray suit of tweeds, with a cloth cap. He wore gaiters, and carried a heavy stick with a knob to it. She was most impressed, however, by the extreme pallor of his face and by the nervousness of his manner. His age, she thought, would be rather over thirty than under it.

"'Can you tell me where I am?' he asked. 'I had almost made up my mind to sleep on the moor, when I saw the light of your lantern.'

"'You are close to the King's Pyland training-stables,' said she.

"'Oh, indeed! What a stroke of luck!' he cried. 'I understand that a stable-boy sleeps there alone every night. Perhaps that is his supper which you are carrying to him. Now I am sure that you would not be too proud to earn the price of a new dress, would you?' He took a piece of white paper folded up out of his waistcoat pocket. 'See that the boy has this to-night, and you shall have the prettiest frock that money can buy.'

"She was frightened by the earnestness of his manner, and ran past him to the window through which she was accustomed to hand the meals. It was already opened, and Hunter was seated at the small table inside. She had begun to tell him of what had happened, when the stranger came up again.

"'Good-evening,' said he, looking through the window. 'I wanted to have a word with you.' The girl has sworn that as he spoke, she noticed the corner of the little paper packet protruding from his closed hand.

"'What business have you here?' asked the lad.

"'It's business that may put something into your pocket,' said the other. 'You've two horses in for the Wessex Cup -- Silver Blaze and Bayard. Let me have the straight tip and you won't be a loser. Is it a fact that at the weights Bayard could give the other a hundred yards in five furlongs, and that the stable have put their money on him?'

"'So, you're one of those damned touts!' cried the lad. 'I'll show you how we serve them in King's Pyland.' He sprang up and rushed across the stable to unloose the dog. The girl fled away to the house, but as she ran, she looked back and saw that the stranger was leaning through the window. A minute later, however, when Hunter rushed out with the hound he was gone, and though he ran all round the buildings, he failed to find any trace of him."

"One moment," I asked. "Did the stable-boy, when he ran out with the dog, leave the door unlocked behind him?"

"Excellent, Watson, excellent!" murmured my companion. "The importance of the point struck me so forcibly that I sent a special wire to Dartmoor yesterday to clear the matter up. The boy locked the door before he left it. The window, I may add, was not large enough for a man to get through.

"Hunter waited until his fellow-grooms had returned, when he sent a message to the trainer and told him what had occurred. Straker was excited at hearing the account, although he does not seem to have quite realized its true significance. It left him, however, vaguely uneasy, and Mrs. Straker, waking at one in the morning, found that he was dressing. In reply to her inquiries, he said that he could not sleep on account of his anxiety about the horses, and that he intended to walk down to the stables to see that all was well. She begged him to remain at home, as she could hear the rain pattering against the window, but in spite of her entreaties he pulled on his large mackintosh and left the house.

"Mrs. Straker awoke at seven in the morning, to find that her husband had not yet returned. She dressed herself hastily, called the maid, and set off for the stables. The door was open; inside, huddled together upon a chair, Hunter was sunk in a state of absolute stupor, the favorite's stall was empty, and there were no signs of his trainer.

"The two lads who slept in the chaff-cutting loft above the harness-room were quickly aroused. They had heard nothing during the night, for they are both sound sleepers. Hunter was obviously under the influence of some powerful drug, and as no sense could be got out of him, he was left to sleep it off while the two lads and the two women ran out in search of the absentees. They still had hopes that the trainer had for some reason taken out the horse for early exercise, but on ascending the knoll near the house, from which all the neighboring moors were visible, they not only could see no signs of the missing favorite, but they perceived something which warned them that they were in the presence of a tragedy.

"About a quarter of a mile from the stables John Straker's overcoat was flapping from a furze-bush. Immediately beyond there was a bowl-shaped depression in the moor, and at the bottom of this was found the dead body of the unfortunate trainer. His head had been shattered by a savage blow from some heavy weapon, and he was wounded on the thigh, where there was a long, clean cut, inflicted evidently by some very sharp instrument. It was clear, however, that Straker had defended himself vigorously against his assailants, for in his right hand he held a small knife, which was clotted with blood up to the handle, while in his left he clasped a red and black silk cravat, which was recognized by the maid as having been worn on the preceding evening by the stranger who had visited the stables. Hunter, on recovering from his stupor, was also quite positive as to the ownership of the cravat. He was equally certain that the same stranger had, while standing at the window, drugged his curried mutton, and so deprived the stables of their watchman. As to the missing horse, there were abundant proofs in the mud which lay at the bottom of the fatal hollow that he had been there at the time of the struggle. But from that morning, he has disappeared, and although a large reward has been offered, and all the gypsies of Dartmoor are on the alert, no news has come of him. Finally, an analysis has shown that the remains of his supper left by the stable-lad contain an appreciable quantity of powdered opium, while the people at the house partook of the same dish on the same night without any ill effect.

"Those are the main facts of the case, stripped of all surmise, and stated as baldly as possible. I shall now recapitulate what the police have done in the matter.

"Inspector Gregory, to whom the case has been committed, is an extremely competent officer. Were he but gifted with imagination he might rise to great heights in his profession. On his arrival, he promptly found and arrested the man upon whom suspicion naturally rested. There was little difficulty in finding him, for he inhabited one of those villas which I have mentioned. His name, it appears, was Fitzroy Simpson. He was a man of excellent birth and education, who had squandered a fortune upon the turf, and who lived now by doing a little quiet and genteel book-making in the sporting clubs of London. An examination of his betting-book shows that bets to the amount of five thousand pounds had been registered by him against the favorite. On being arrested, he volunteered that statement that he had come down to Dartmoor in the hope of getting some information about the King's Pyland horses, and also about Desborough, the second favorite, which was in charge of Silas Brown at the Mapleton stables. He did not attempt to deny that he had acted as described upon the evening before, but declared that he had no sinister designs, and had simply wished to obtain first-hand information. When confronted with his cravat, he turned very pale, and was utterly unable to account for its presence in the hand of the murdered man. His wet clothing showed that he had been out in the storm of the night before, and his stick, which was a Penang-lawyer weighted with lead, was just such a weapon as might, by repeated blows, have inflicted the terrible injuries to which the trainer had succumbed. On the other hand, there was no wound upon his person, while the state of Straker's knife would show that one at least of his assailants must bear his mark upon him. There you have it all in a nutshell, Watson, and if you can give me any light I shall be infinitely obliged to you."

I had listened with the greatest interest to the statement which Holmes, with characteristic clearness, had laid before me. Though most of the facts were familiar to me, I had not sufficiently appreciated their relative importance, nor their connection to each other.

"Is in not possible," I suggested, "that the incised would upon Straker may have been caused by his own knife in the convulsive struggles which follow any brain injury?"

"It is more than possible; it is probable," said Holmes. "In that case, one of the main points in favor of the accused disappears."

"And yet," said I, "even now I fail to understand what the theory of the police can be."

"I am afraid that whatever theory we state has very grave objections to it," returned my companion. "The police imagine, I take it, that this Fitzroy Simpson, having drugged the lad, and having in some way obtained a duplicate key, opened the stable door and took out the horse, with the intention, apparently, of kidnapping him altogether. His bridle is missing, so that Simpson must have put this on. Then, having left the door open behind him, he was leading the horse away over the moor, when he was either met or overtaken by the trainer. A row naturally ensued. Simpson beat out the trainer's brains with his heavy stick without receiving any injury from the small knife which Straker used in self-defence, and then the thief either led the horse on to some secret hiding-place, or else it may have bolted during the struggle, and be now wandering out on the moors. That is the case as it appears to the police, and improbable as it is, all other explanations are more improbable still. However, I shall very quickly test the matter when I am once upon the spot, and until then I cannot really see how we can get much further than our present position."

It was evening before we reached the little town of Tavistock, which lies, like the boss of a shield, in the middle of the huge circle of Dartmoor. Two gentlemen were awaiting us in the station -- the one a tall, fair man with lion-like hair and beard and curiously penetrating light blue eyes; the other a small, alert person, very neat and dapper, in a frock-coat and gaiters, with trim little side-whiskers and an eye-glass. The latter was Colonel Ross, the well-known sportsman; the other, Inspector Gregory, a man who was rapidly making his name in the English detective service.

"I am delighted that you have come down, Mr. Holmes," said the Colonel. "The Inspector here has done all that could possibly be suggested, but I wish to leave no stone unturned in trying to avenge poor Straker and in recovering my horse."

"Have there been any fresh developments?" asked Holmes.

"I am sorry to say that we have made very little progress," said the Inspector. "We have an open carriage outside, and as you would no doubt like to see the place before the light fails, we might talk it over as we drive."

A minute later we were all seated in a comfortable landau, and were rattling through the quaint old Devonshire city. Inspector Gregory was full of his case, and poured out a stream of remarks, while Holmes threw in an occasional question or interjection. Colonel Ross leaned back with his arms folded and his hat tilted over his eyes, while I listened with interest to the dialogue of the two detectives. Gregory was formulating his theory, which was almost exactly what Holmes had foretold in the train.

"The net is drawn pretty close round Fitzroy Simpson," he remarked, "and I believe myself that he is our man. At the same time, I recognize that the evidence is purely circumstantial, and that some new development may upset it."

"How about Straker's knife?"

"We have quite come to the conclusion that he wounded himself in his fall."

"My friend Dr. Watson made that suggestion to me as we came down. If so, it would tell against this man Simpson."

"Undoubtedly. He has neither a knife nor any sign of a wound. The evidence against him is certainly very strong. He had a great interest in the disappearance of the favorite. He lies under suspicion of having poisoned the stable-boy, he was undoubtedly out in the storm, he was armed with a heavy stick, and his cravat was found in the dead man's hand. I really think we have enough to go before a jury."

Holmes shook his head. "A clever counsel would tear it all to rags," said he. "Why should he take the horse out of the stable? If he wished to injure it why could he not do it there? Has a duplicate key been found in his possession? What chemist sold him the powdered opium? Above all, where could he, a stranger to the district, hide a horse, and such a horse as this? What is his own explanation as to the paper which he wished the maid to give to the stable-boy?"

"He says that it was a ten-pound note. One was found in his purse. But your other difficulties are not so formidable as they seem. He is not a stranger to the district. He has twice lodged at Tavistock in the summer. The opium was probably brought from London. The key, having served its purpose, would be hurled away. The horse may be at the bottom of one of the pits or old mines upon the moor."

"What does he say about the cravat?"

"He acknowledges that it is his, and declares that he had lost it. But a new element has been introduced into the case which may account for his leading the horse from the stable."

Holmes pricked up his ears.

"We have found traces which show that a party of gypsies encamped on Monday night within a mile of the spot where the murder took place. On Tuesday, they were gone. Now, presuming that there was some understanding between Simpson and these gypsies, might he not have been leading the horse to them when he was overtaken, and may they not have him now?"

"It is certainly possible."

"The moor is being scoured for these gypsies. I have also examined every stable and out-house in Tavistock, and for a radius of ten miles."

"There is another training-stable quite close, I understand?"

"Yes, and that is a factor which we must certainly not neglect. As Desborough, their horse, was second in the betting, they had an interest in the disappearance of the favorite. Silas Brown, the trainer, is known to have had large bets upon the event, and he was no friend to poor Straker. We have, however, examined the stables, and there is nothing to connect him with the affair."

"And nothing to connect this man Simpson with the interests of the Mapleton stables?"

"Nothing at all."

Holmes leaned back in the carriage, and the conversation ceased. A few minutes later our driver pulled up at a neat little red-brick villa with overhanging eaves which stood by the road. Some distance off, across a paddock, lay a long gray-tiled out-building. In every other direction the low curves of the moor, bronze-colored from the fading ferns, stretched away to the sky-line, broken only by the steeples of Tavistock, and by a cluster of houses away to the westward which marked the Mapleton stables. We all sprang out with the exception of Holmes, who continued to lean back with his eyes fixed upon the sky in front of him, entirely absorbed in his own thoughts. It was only when I touched his arm that he roused himself with a violent start and stepped out of the carriage.

"Excuse me," said he, turning to Colonel Ross, who had looked at him in some surprise. "I was day-dreaming." There was a gleam in his eyes and a suppressed excitement in his manner which convinced me, used as I was to his ways, that his hand was upon a clue, though I could not imagine where he had found it.

"Perhaps you would prefer at once to go on to the scene of the crime, Mr. Holmes?" said Gregory.

"I think that I should prefer to stay here a little and go into one or two questions of detail. Straker was brought back here, I presume?"

"Yes; he lies upstairs. The inquest is to-morrow."

"He has been in your service some years, Colonel Ross?"

"I have always found him an excellent servant."

"I presume that you made an inventory of what he had in this pockets at the time of his death, Inspector?"

"I have the things themselves in the sitting-room, if you would care to see them."

"I should be very glad." We all filed into the front room and sat round the central table while the Inspector unlocked a square tin box and laid a small heap of things before us. There was a box of vestas, two inches of tallow candle, an A D P brier-root pipe, a pouch of seal-skin with half an ounce of long-cut Cavendish, a silver watch with a gold chain, five sovereigns in gold, an aluminum pencil-case, a few papers, and an ivory-handled knife with a very delicate, inflexible bade marked Weiss & Co., London.

"This is a very singular knife," said Holmes, lifting it up and examining it minutely. "I presume, as I see blood-stains upon it, that it is the one which was found in the dead man's grasp. Watson, this knife is surely in your line?"

"It is what we call a cataract knife," said I.

"I thought so. A very delicate blade devised for very delicate work. A strange thing for a man to carry with him upon a rough expedition, especially as it would not shut in his pocket."

"The tip was guarded by a disk of cork which we found beside his body," said the Inspector. "His wife tells us that the knife had lain upon the dressing-table, and that he had picked it up as he left the room. It was a poor weapon, but perhaps the best that he could lay his hands on at the moment."

"Very possible. How about these papers?"

"Three of them are receipted hay-dealers' accounts. One of them is a letter of instructions from Colonel Ross. This other is a milliner's account for thirty-seven pounds fifteen made out by Madame Lesurier, of Bond Street, to William Derbyshire. Mrs. Straker tells us that Derbyshire was a friend of her husband's and that occasionally his letters were addressed here."

"Madam Derbyshire had somewhat expensive tastes," remarked Holmes, glancing down the account. "Twenty-two guineas is rather heavy for a single costume. However there appears to be nothing more to learn, and we may now go down to the scene of the crime."

As we emerged from the sitting-room a woman, who had been waiting in the passage, took a step forward and laid her hand upon the Inspector's sleeve. Her face was haggard and thin and eager, stamped with the print of a recent horror.

"Have you got them? Have you found them?" she panted.

"No, Mrs. Straker. But Mr. Holmes here has come from London to help us, and we shall do all that is possible."

"Surely I met you in Plymouth at a garden-party some little time ago, Mrs. Straker?" said Holmes.

"No, sir; you are mistaken."

"Dear me! Why, I could have sworn to it. You wore a costume of dove-colored silk with ostrich-feather trimming."

"I never had such a dress, sir," answered the lady.

"Ah, that quite settles it," said Holmes. And with an apology, he followed the Inspector outside. A short walk across the moor took us to the hollow in which the body had been found. At the brink of it was the furze-bush upon which the coat had been hung.

"There was no wind that night, I understand," said Holmes.

"None; but very heavy rain."

"In that case, the overcoat was not blown against the furze-bush, but placed there."

"Yes, it was laid across the bush."

"You fill me with interest, I perceive that the ground has been trampled up a good deal. No doubt many feet have been here since Monday night."

"A piece of matting has been laid here at the side, and we have all stood upon that."

"Excellent."

"In this bag I have one of the boots which Straker wore, one of Fitzroy Simpson's shoes, and a cast horseshoe of Silver Blaze."

"My dear Inspector, you surpass yourself!" Homes took the bag, and, descending into the hollow, he pushed the matting into a more central position. Then stretching himself upon his face and leaning his chin upon his hands, he made a careful study of the trampled mud in front of him. "Hullo!" said he, suddenly. "What's this?" It was a wax vesta half burned, which was so coated with mud that it looked at first like a little chip of wood.

"I cannot think how I came to overlook it," said the Inspector, with an expression of annoyance.

"It was invisible, buried in the mud. I only saw it because I was looking for it."

"What! You expected to find it?"

"I thought it not unlikely."

He took the boots from the bag, and compared the impressions of each of them with marks upon the ground. Then he clambered up to the rim of the hollow, and crawled about among the ferns and bushes.

"I am afraid that there are no more tracks," said the Inspector. "I have examined the ground very carefully for a hundred yards in each direction."

"Indeed!" said Holmes, rising. "I should not have the impertinence to do it again after what you say. But I should like to take a little walk over the moor before it grows dark, that I may know my ground to-morrow, and I think that I shall put this horseshoe into my pocket for luck."

Colonel Ross, who had shown some signs of impatience at my companion's quiet and systematic method of work, glanced at his watch. "I wish you would come back with me, Inspector," said he. "There are several points on which I should like your advice, and especially as to whether we do not owe it to the public to remove our horse's name from the entries for the Cup."

"Certainly not," cried Holmes, with decision. "I should let the name stand."

The Colonel bowed. "I am very glad to have had your opinion, sir," said he. "You will find us at poor Straker's house when you have finished your walk, and we can drive together into Tavistock."

He turned back with the Inspector, while Holmes and I walked slowly across the moor. The sun was beginning to sink behind the stables of Mapleton, and the long, sloping plain in front of us was tinged with gold, deepening into rich, ruddy browns where the faded ferns and brambles caught the evening light. But the glories of the landscape were all wasted upon my companion, who was sunk in the deepest thought.

"It's this way, Watson," said he at last. "We may leave the question of who killed John Straker for the instant, and confine ourselves to finding out what has become of the horse. Now, supposing that he broke away during or after the tragedy, where could he have gone to? The horse is a very gregarious creature. If left to himself his instincts would have been either to return to King's Pyland or go over to Mapleton. Why should he run wild upon the moor? He would surely have been seen by now. And why should gypsies kidnap him? These people always clear out when they hear of trouble, for they do not wish to be pestered by the police. They could

174

not hope to sell such a horse. They would run a great risk and gain nothing by taking him. Surely that is clear."

"Where is he, then?"

"I have already said that he must have gone to King's Pyland or to Mapleton. He is not at King's Pyland. Therefore, he is at Mapleton. Let us take that as a working hypothesis and see what it leads us to. This part of the moor, as the Inspector remarked, is very hard and dry. But if falls away towards Mapleton, and you can see from here that there is a long hollow over yonder, which must have been very wet on Monday night. If our supposition is correct, then the horse must have crossed that, and there is the point where we should look for his tracks."

We had been walking briskly during this conversation, and a few more minutes brought us to the hollow in question. At Holmes' request, I walked down the bank to the right, and he to the left, but I had not taken fifty paces before I heard him give a shout, and saw him waving his hand to me. The track of a horse was plainly outlined in the soft earth in front of him, and the shoe which he took from his pocket exactly fitted the impression.

"See the value of imagination," said Holmes. "It is the one quality which Gregory lacks. We imagined what might have happened, acted upon the supposition, and find ourselves justified. Let us proceed."

We crossed the marshy bottom and passed over a quarter of a mile of dry, hard turf. Again the ground sloped, and again we came on the tracks. Then we lost them for half a mile, but only to pick them up once more quite close to Mapleton. It was Holmes who saw them first, and he stood pointing with a look of triumph upon his face. A man's track was visible beside the horse's.

"The horse was alone before," I cried.

"Quite so. It was alone before. Hullo, what is this?"

The double track turned sharp off and took the direction of King's Pyland. Homes whistled, and we both followed along after it.

His eyes were on the trail, but I happened to look a little to one side, and saw to my surprise the same tracks coming back again in the opposite direction.

"One for you, Watson," said Holmes, when I pointed it out. "You have saved us a long walk, which would have brought us back on our own traces. Let us follow the return track."

We had not to go far. It ended at the paving of asphalt which led up to the gates of the Mapleton stables. As we approached, a groom ran out from them.

"We don't want any loiterers about here," said he.

"I only wished to ask a question," said Holmes, with his finger and thumb in his waistcoat pocket. "Should I be too early to see your master, Mr. Silas Brown, if I were to call at five o'clock to-morrow morning?"

"Bless you, sir, if any one is about he will be, for he is always the first stirring. But here he is, sir, to answer your questions for himself. No, sir, no; it is as much as my place is worth to let him see me touch your money. Afterwards, if you like."

As Sherlock Holmes replaced the half-crown which he had drawn from his pocket, a fierce-looking elderly man strode out from the gate with a hunting-crop swinging in his hand.

"What's this, Dawson!" he cried. "No gossiping! Go about your business! And you, what the devil do you want here?"

"Ten minutes' talk with you, my good sir," said Holmes in the sweetest of voices.

"I've no time to talk to every gadabout. We want no stranger here. Be off, or you may find a dog at your heels."

Holmes leaned forward and whispered something in the trainer's ear. He started violently and flushed to the temples.

"It's a lie!" he shouted, "an infernal lie!"

"Very good. Shall we argue about it here in public or talk it over in your parlor?"

"Oh, come in if you wish to."

Holmes smiled. "I shall not keep you more than a few minutes, Watson," said he. "Now, Mr. Brown, I am quite at your disposal."

It was twenty minutes, and the reds had all faded into grays before Holmes and the trainer reappeared. Never have I seen such a change as had been brought about in Silas Brown in that short time. His face was ashy pale, beads of perspiration shone upon his brow, and his hands shook until the hunting-crop wagged like a branch in the wind. His bullying, overbearing manner was all gone too, and he cringed along at my companion's side like a dog with its master.

"You instructions will be done. It shall all be done," said he.

"There must be no mistake," said Holmes, looking round at him. The other winced as he read the menace in his eyes.

"Oh no, there shall be no mistake. It shall be there. Should I change it first or not?"

Holmes thought a little and then burst out laughing. "No, don't," said he; "I shall write to you about it. No tricks, now, or --"

"Oh, you can trust me, you can trust me!"

"Yes, I think I can. Well, you shall hear from me to-morrow." He turned upon his heel, disregarding the trembling hand which the other held out to him, and we set off for King's Pyland.

"A more perfect compound of the bully, coward, and sneak than Master Silas Brown I have seldom met with," remarked Holmes as we trudged along together.

"He has the horse, then?"

"He tried to bluster out of it, but I described to him so exactly what his actions had been upon that morning that he is convinced that I was watching him. Of course, you observed the peculiarly square toes in the impressions, and that his own boots exactly corresponded to them. Again, of course, no subordinate would have dared to do such a thing. I described to him how, when according to his custom he was the first down, he perceived a strange horse wandering over the moor. How he went out to it, and his astonishment at recognizing, from the white forehead which has given the favorite its name, that chance had put in his power the only horse which could beat the one upon which he had put his money. Then I described how his first impulse had been to lead him back to King's Pyland, and how the devil had shown him how he could hide the horse until the race was over, and how he had led it back and concealed it at Mapleton. When I told him every detail he gave it up and thought only of saving his own skin."

"But his stables had been searched?"

"Oh, an old horse-fakir like him has many a dodge."

"But are you not afraid to leave the horse in his power now, since he has every interest in injuring it?"

"My dear fellow, he will guard it as the apple of his eye. He knows that his only hope of mercy is to produce it safe."

"Colonel Ross did not impress me as a man who would be likely to show much mercy in any case."

"The matter does not rest with Colonel Ross. I follow my own methods, and tell as much or as little as I choose. That is the advantage of being unofficial. I don't know whether you observed it, Watson, but the Colonel's manner has been just a trifle cavalier to me. I am inclined now to have a little amusement at his expense. Say nothing to him about the horse."

"Certainly not without your permission."

"And of course, this is all quite a minor point compared to the question of who killed John Straker."

"And you will devote yourself to that?"

"On the contrary, we both go back to London by the night train."

I was thunderstruck by my friend's words. We had only been a few hours in Devonshire, and that he should give up an investigation which he had begun so brilliantly was quite incomprehensible to me. Not a word more could I draw from him until we were back at the trainer's house. The Colonel and the Inspector were awaiting us in the parlor.

"My friend and I return to town by the night-express," said Holmes. "We have had a charming little breath of your beautiful Dartmoor air."

The Inspector opened his eyes, and the Colonel's lip curled in a sneer.

"So you despair of arresting the murderer of poor Straker," said he.

Holmes shrugged his shoulders. "There are certainly grave difficulties in the way," said he. "I have every hope, however, that your horse will start upon Tuesday, and I beg that you will have your jockey in readiness. Might I ask for a photograph of Mr. John Straker?"

The Inspector took one from an envelope and handed it to him.

"My dear Gregory, you anticipate all my wants. If I might ask you to wait here for an instant, I have a question which I should like to put to the maid."

"I must say that I am rather disappointed in our London consultant," said Colonel Ross, bluntly, as my friend left the room. "I do not see that we are any further than when he came."

"At least, you have his assurance that your horse will run," said I.

"Yes, I have his assurance," said the Colonel, with a shrug of his shoulders. "I should prefer to have the horse."

I was about to make some reply in defence of my friend when he entered the room again.

"Now, gentlemen," said he, "I am quite ready for Tavistock."

As we stepped into the carriage, one of the stable-lads held the door open for us. A sudden idea seemed to occur to Holmes, for he leaned forward and touched the lad upon the sleeve.

"You have a few sheep in the paddock," he said. "Who attends to them?"

"I do, sir."

"Have you noticed anything amiss with them of late?"

"Well, sir, not of much account; but three of them have gone lame, sir."

I could see that Holmes was extremely pleased, for he chuckled and rubbed his hands together.

"A long shot, Watson; a very long shot," said he, pinching my arm. "Gregory, let me recommend to your attention this singular epidemic among the sheep. Drive on, coachman!"

Colonel Ross still wore an expression which showed the poor opinion which he had formed of my companion's ability, but I saw by the Inspector's face that his attention had been keenly aroused.

"You consider that to be important?" he asked.

"Exceedingly so."

"Is there any point to which you would wish to draw my attention?"

"To the curious incident of the dog in the night-time."

"The dog did nothing in the night-time."

"That was the curious incident," remarked Sherlock Holmes.

Four days later Holmes and I were again in the train, bound for Winchester to see the race for the Wessex Cup. Colonel Ross met us by appointment outside the station, and we drove in his drag to the course beyond the town. His face was grave, and his manner was cold in the extreme.

"I have seen nothing of my horse," said he.

"I suppose that you would know him when you saw him?" asked Holmes.

The Colonel was very angry. "I have been on the turf for twenty years, and never was asked such a question as that before," said he. "A child would know Silver Blaze, with his white forehead and his mottled off-foreleg."

"How is the betting?"

"Well, that is the curious part of it. You could have got fifteen to one yesterday, but the price has become shorter and shorter, until you can hardly get three to one now."

"Hum!" said Holmes. "Somebody knows something, that is clear."

As the drag drew up in the enclosure near the grand stand, I glanced at the card to see the entries.

Wessex Plate [it ran] 50 sovs each h ft with 1000 sovs added for four and five-year-olds. Second, L300. Third, L200. New course (one mile and five furlongs). Mr. Heath Newton's The Negro. Red cap. Cinnamon jacket. Colonel Wardlaw's Pugilist. Pink cap. Blue and black jacket. Lord Backwater's Desborough. Yellow cap and sleeves. Colonel Ross's Silver Blaze. Black cap. Red jacket. Duke of Balmoral's Iris. Yellow and black stripes. Lord Singleford's Rasper. Purple cap. Black sleeves.

"We scratched our other one, and put all hopes on your word," said the Colonel. "Why, what is that? Silver Blaze favorite?"

"Five to four against Silver Blaze!" roared the ring. "Five to four against Silver Blaze! Five to fifteen against Desborough! Five to four on the field!"

"There are the numbers up," I cried. "They are all six there."

"All six there? Then my horse is running," cried the Colonel in great agitation. "But I don't see him. My colors have not passed."

"Only five have passed. This must be he."

As I spoke a powerful bay horse swept out from the weighting enclosure and cantered past us, bearing on it back the well-known black and red of the Colonel.

"That's not my horse," cried the owner. "That beast has not a white hair upon its body. What is this that you have done, Mr. Holmes?"

"Well, well, let us see how he gets on," said my friend, imperturbably. For a few minutes, he gazed through my field-glass. "Capital! An excellent start!" he cried suddenly. "There they are, coming round the curve!"

From our drag, we had a superb view as they came up the straight. The six horses were so close together that a carpet could have covered them, but half way up the yellow of the Mapleton stable showed to the front. Before they reached us, however, Desborough's bolt was shot, and the Colonel's horse, coming away with a rush, passed the post a good six lengths before its rival, the Duke of Balmoral's Iris making a bad third.

"It's my race, anyhow," gasped the Colonel, passing his hand over his eyes. "I confess that I can make neither head nor tail of it. Don't you think that you have kept up your mystery long enough, Mr. Holmes?"

"Certainly, Colonel, you shall know everything. Let us all go round and have a look at the horse together. Here he is," he continued, as we made our way into the weighing enclosure, where only owners and their friends find admittance. "You have only to wash his face and his leg in spirits of wine, and you will find that he is the same old Silver Blaze as ever."

"You take my breath away!"

"I found him in the hands of a fakir, and took the liberty of running him just as he was sent over."

"My dear sir, you have done wonders. The horse looks very fit and well. It never went better in its life. I owe you a thousand apologies for having doubted your ability. You have done me a great service by recovering my horse. You would do me a greater still if you could lay your hands on the murderer of John Straker."

"I have done so," said Holmes quietly.

The Colonel and I stared at him in amazement. "You have got him! Where is he, then?"

"He is here."

"Here! Where?"

"In my company at the present moment."

The Colonel flushed angrily. "I quite recognize that I am under obligations to you, Mr. Holmes," said he, "but I must regard what you have just said as either a very bad joke or an insult."

Sherlock Holmes laughed. "I assure you that I have not associated you with the crime, Colonel," said he. "The real murderer is standing immediately behind you." He stepped past and laid his hand upon the glossy neck of the thoroughbred.

"The horse!" cried both the Colonel and myself.

"Yes, the horse. And it may lessen his guilt if I say that it was done in self-defence, and that John Straker was a man who was entirely unworthy of your confidence. But there goes the bell, and as I stand to win a little on this next race, I shall defer a lengthy explanation until a more fitting time."

We had the corner of a Pullman car to ourselves that evening as we whirled back to London, and I fancy that the journey was a short one to Colonel Ross as well as to myself, as we listened to our companion's narrative of the events which had occurred at the Dartmoor training-stables upon the Monday night, and the means by which he had unravelled them.

"I confess," said he, "that any theories which I had formed from the newspaper reports were entirely erroneous. And yet there were indications there, had they not been overlaid by other details which concealed their true import. I went to Devonshire with the conviction that Fitzroy Simpson was the true culprit, although, of course, I saw that the evidence against him was by no means complete. It was while I was in the carriage, just as we reached the trainer's house, that the immense significance of the curried mutton occurred to me. You may remember that I was distrait, and remained sitting after you had all alighted. I was marvelling in my own mind how I could possibly have overlooked so obvious a clue."

"I confess," said the Colonel, "that even now I cannot see how it helps us."

"It was the first link in my chain of reasoning. Powdered opium is by no means tasteless. The flavor is not disagreeable, but it is perceptible. Were it mixed with any ordinary dish the eater would undoubtedly detect it, and would probably eat no more. A curry was exactly the medium which would disguise this taste. By no possible supposition could this stranger, Fitzroy Simpson, have caused curry to be served in the trainer's family that night, and it is surely too monstrous a coincidence to suppose that he happened to come along with powdered opium upon the very night when a dish happened to be served which would disguise the flavor. That is unthinkable. Therefore, Simpson becomes eliminated from the case, and our attention centers upon Straker and his wife, the only two people who could have chosen curried mutton for supper that night. The opium was added after the dish was set aside for the stable-boy, for the others had the same for supper with no ill effects. Which of them, then, had access to that dish without the maid seeing them?

"Before deciding that question I had grasped the significance of the silence of the dog, for one true inference invariably suggests others. The Simpson incident had shown me that a dog was kept in the stables, and yet, though some one had been in and had fetched out a horse, he had not barked enough to arouse the two lads in the loft. Obviously, the midnight visitor was some one whom the dog knew well.

"I was already convinced, or almost convinced, that John Straker went down to the stables in the dead of the night and took out Silver Blaze. For what purpose? For a dishonest one, obviously, or why should he drug his own stable-boy? And yet I was at a loss to know why. There have been cases before now where trainers have made sure of great sums of money by laying against their own horses, through agents, and then preventing them from winning by fraud. Sometimes it is a pulling jockey. Sometimes it is some surer and subtler means. What was it here? I hoped that the contents of his pockets might help me to form a conclusion.

"And they did so. You cannot have forgotten the singular knife which was found in the dead man's hand, a knife which certainly no sane man would choose for a weapon. It was, as Dr. Watson told us, a form of knife which is used for the most delicate operations known in surgery. And it was to be used for a delicate operation that night. You must know, with your wide experience of turf matters, Colonel Ross, that it is possible to make a slight nick upon the tendons of a horse's ham, and to do it subcutaneously, so as to leave absolutely no trace. A horse so treated would develop a slight lameness, which would be put down to a strain in exercise or a touch of rheumatism, but never to foul play."

"Villain! Scoundrel!" cried the Colonel.

"We have here the explanation of why John Straker wished to take the horse out on to the moor. So spirited a creature would have certainly roused the soundest of sleepers when it felt the prick of the knife. It was absolutely necessary to do it in the open air."

"I have been blind!" cried the Colonel. "Of course, that was why he needed the candle, and struck the match."

"Undoubtedly. But in examining his belongings I was fortunate enough to discover not only the method of the crime, but even its motives. As a man of the world, Colonel, you know that men do not

185

carry other people's bills about in their pockets. We have most of us quite enough to do to settle our own. I at once concluded that Straker was leading a double life, and keeping a second establishment. The nature of the bill showed that there was a lady in the case, and one who had expensive tastes. Liberal as you are with your servants, one can hardly expect that they can buy twenty-guinea walking dresses for their ladies. I questioned Mrs. Straker as to the dress without her knowing it, and having satisfied myself that it had never reached her, I made a note of the milliner's address, and felt that by calling there with Straker's photograph I could easily dispose of the mythical Derbyshire.

"From that time on all was plain. Straker had led out the horse to a hollow where his light would be invisible. Simpson in his flight had dropped his cravat, and Straker had picked it up -- with some idea, perhaps, that he might use it in securing the horse's leg. Once in the hollow, he had got behind the horse and had struck a light; but the creature frightened at the sudden glare, and with the strange instinct of animals feeling that some mischief was intended, had lashed out, and the steel shoe had struck Straker full on the forehead. He had already, in spite of the rain, taken off his overcoat in order to do his delicate task, and so, as he fell, his knife gashed his thigh. Do I make it clear?"

"Wonderful!" cried the Colonel. "Wonderful! You might have been there!"

"My final shot was, I confess a very long one. It struck me that so astute a man as Straker would not undertake this delicate tendon-nicking without a little practice. What could he practice on? My eyes fell upon the sheep, and I asked a question which, rather to my surprise, showed that my surmise was correct.

"When I returned to London I called upon the milliner, who had recognized Straker as an excellent customer of the name of Derbyshire, who had a very dashing wife, with a strong partiality for expensive dresses. I have no doubt that this woman had plunged him over head and ears in debt, and so led him into this miserable plot."

"You have explained all but one thing," cried the Colonel. "Where was the horse?"

"Ah, it bolted, and was cared for by one of your neighbors. We must have an amnesty in that direction, I think. This is Clapham Junction, if I am not mistaken, and we shall be in Victoria in less than ten minutes. If you care to smoke a cigar in our rooms, Colonel, I shall be happy to give you any other details which might interest you."

Made in United States
North Haven, CT
24 July 2022